MW01283666

Romance Unbound Publishing

Secrets
BDSM Connections
Book 1

Claire Thompson

Edited by
Donna Fisk, Jae Ashley

Cover Art by
Mayhem Cover Creations
Fine Line Edit by Kathy Kozakewich

Print ISBN 978-1535362924

CHAPTER 1

The rope around Allie's wrists was tight, her arms pulled taut and secured to the headboard. His hard body covered hers, his cock pummeling insistently inside her. The foreplay had been, if not quite as intense as she liked, certainly spicy, with plenty of spanking, nipple torture, clit teasing and even a good, thuddy flogging.

He had almost, though not quite, sent her flying as the whip licked and kissed her skin, the intensity increasing as he got more and more excited. *Yes, yes, yes, yes,* she'd silently shouted as the pain edged in that magical way toward something powerful and sublime. Allie had only experienced that kind of pure, ecstatic release that comes from handling, overcoming and finally embracing erotic pain once or twice in the scene, but it had been enough to keep her coming back for more.

He'd quit just before the miracle, though he'd seemed entirely unaware of what he'd done, or rather, failed to do, and Allie hadn't told him. In her mind, if you had to tell them, then the connection wasn't there, no matter how much you wished it could be.

"I own you." He thrust hard inside her. She shifted, trying to find a better angle. He took that as a positive sign. "Yeah, that's it, I'm going to make you come so hard, babe. You belong to me. I am your Master, to do with as I will."

Okay, so he'd been reading too many bad erotic novels, or, more likely watching too much lousy BDSM porn online, but at least he was trying. The guy was sincere, if a little overbearing, and he appeared to be nearly as into her as he was into himself.

He pounded away, his breath rasping in his throat, his heart thumping beneath his sweat-slicked skin. His stroke was good now, tapping at her sweet spot from the inside out. Maybe, just maybe, it would be enough?

"Come on, slave girl," he gasped. "I can feel it—you're almost there. No one can resist Master Gene. Come for me. I order you to come." He swiveled and thrust, urgency radiating from him like heat. "Do it. Now."

Give him what he wants. You can do it. Meg Ryan has nothing on you.

Allie moaned and arched her hips upward. She began to pant. "Oh, oh, oh, oh! Yes, yes, yes!" She shuddered and stiffened, gripping him hard with her thighs. She squinted through slitted eyelids to peer at his face looming over hers. His eyes were squeezed shut, his head thrown back, the tendons on his neck distended as he hammered her into the mattress. She continued to sigh and moan in syncopated rhythm to his orgasmic cries.

Finally he lay still, the steady beat of his heart against hers the only sign of life. He was heavy and limp on top of her. The tip of Allie's nose was itchy and her right calf was cramping. She longed to shove him off her. She wished fervently the ropes around her now chafed wrists would miraculously evaporate. She desperately needed a shower and a cold drink, preferably something eighty proof.

Allie closed her eyes and uttered a small, silent wish: *disappear.*

It didn't work.

Finally he lifted himself on his elbows and peered down into her face. "Hey, you. You alive? I told you I'd make you come. Master Gene knows how to treat a sub girl, huh?" He grinned, the pride evident on his handsome face.

Allie smiled back and sighed, letting him interpret the sound as she knew he would. "Oh, yeah," she breathed. "Thank you, Sir."

"You're welcome, sub girl."

"Come on. I don't want to go alone. It's a really cool new private dungeon in Newton and the party starts at nine. You know I don't like to drive at night."

"Newton? I didn't know they went in for things like that in the suburbs."

"Hey, Boston doesn't have a monopoly on BDSM, just because you never like to leave the city," Lauren retorted, though she was grinning. "It'll be fun. You could invite that guy you met at that munch thing, what was his name? He was a real hunk. Reminded me of Justin Timberlake. Total masturbatory material." Without giving Allie a chance to reply, Lauren continued in her rapid patter, "It's half price cover for single women, and I heard this dungeon has super high tech, state-of-the-art equipment. Yeah, it's kind of a haul, but my car gets great gas mileage. I'll even pay your cover if you're short on funds. Please? Please say yes. I don't want to go alone." Lauren leaned forward eagerly, her expression comically beseeching.

The waitress came by with their salads and glasses of wine. Allie waited until she'd served them and moved away. "That hunk you referred to is named Gene. We've been talking all week on Facebook. He does have experience in the scene and as far as I could tell wasn't secretly married or gay or anything. We actually hooked up last night."

"Last night? Oh my god, Allie! O-M-fucking-G! You hooked up? Where? Your place? His? A hotel? And you didn't even tell me? Was it fabulous? Was he hot? Did he look as good naked as he did in black leather? Why didn't you call me immediately?"

Allie laughed, at once exasperated and amused by her best friend. She finished chewing a mouthful of salad, took a sip of her wine and then replied. "I didn't tell you yet because you haven't stopped talking since we sat down. He came to my place. He was good, as far as it went."

"Meaning?"

"Meaning he was very good, technically speaking, with the ropes and the flogger, but it was pretty clear for him it was all just foreplay. Like he had a check list of things to do to me so that he could fuck me at the end." Allie held up her hand, using an invisible pen to make checkmarks in the air. "Tie her up? Check. Apply the nipple clamps? Check. Say sexy, dominant things that will get her wet? Check. Smack her ass a bit? Check. Bring out the big scary flogger? Check."

Lauren laughed out loud, and Allie, in spite of herself, joined in.

"I'm sorry. I'm being really mean. The guy was perfectly nice. There just wasn't that connection, you know? That spark."

Lauren nodded supportively, reminding Allie why she was her best friend.

Allie took another long swallow of her wine and continued, "He was into me, but I kind of got the feeling he was into the *idea* of me, more than me, if you know what I mean? He was The Dom and I was The Sub and we were Doing a Scene. I was an extension of him, of his ego, of Master Gene, Dom extraordinaire." Allie lowered her voice as she said Master Gene, drawing quotations around the words with her fingers.

Lauren giggled and then sighed. "Sounds depressingly familiar."

Allie shrugged. "At least he was good eye candy while he performed his masterful repertoire. He's definitely got a killer bod. He has a complex workout regime that I got to hear about in excruciating detail."

Lauren wrinkled her nose in sympathy. "The really hot ones can be a little too into themselves, right? But if he's a real Dom, you can overlook it. I mean"—she hugged herself and closed her eyes, her expression wistful—"I'd give anything to meet Mister Right. I mean Master Right."

She opened her eyes, her expression once more earnestly beseeching. "That's why I want to go to this play party tomorrow night. Martin Haller is going to be there. I heard through the grapevine he broke up with that Lisa chick, and I'll be there, ready and willing to be his rebound sub girl. You should definitely go. You never know, your Master Right could be there, too, waiting to sweep you off your feet and into his dungeon."

"Oh, right," Allie said, letting sarcasm drip through her words. "Like Master Right is really going to be waiting for me at a private dungeon in Newton, Massachusetts. I probably have a better chance to win the lottery."

It was Lauren's turn to shrug. "Hey, you know what they say. You gotta be in it to win it."

Allie blew out a sigh of defeat, though she couldn't help but smile at her friend. "Okay, okay, Lauren. I'll go with you."

Allie sat at the juice bar of Spanked, already wishing she hadn't come. She knew she was sending off *leave me alone* vibes, which had to be why no one had approached her in the half hour or so she'd been brooding at the bar.

Lauren, of course, had immediately gravitated to Martin Haller, whom she'd spotted the moment they'd entered the party. She was now happily ensconced in a private scene room with the guy, no doubt having a blast. Allie envied Lauren, who seemed to sail happily from relationship to relationship, always remaining good friends with prior lovers when she invariably broke up with them.

When Allie had first discovered BDSM in her early twenties, she had been excited to explore the passion of erotic submission. At first she'd been certain she'd finally found that missing link—the thing that would allow her to truly connect with another human being. And while she'd come to crave the intensity and release of erotic suffering and submissive sex, the thick wall of ice around her heart had never fully thawed. Secretly she worried she was broken—incapable of love, destined to remain alone.

"Can I buy you a drink?"

Allie looked up to see a guy of around fifty with a craggy face and deep-set, very blue eyes. He was dressed in the requisite black leather vest and pants, a rather unattractive bulge of fat showing below the vest, which wasn't quite long enough or large enough to hide it. Even though it was a size too small, Allie recognized the quality of the leather and the workmanship. The heavy, gold watch on his wrist probably cost more than she earned in a month.

"Oh, thanks, that's okay. I have one." She held up the clear plastic cup of orange juice over ice. No liquor was allowed at this particular BDSM play party, which was probably good practice, though Allie would have loved a double scotch on the rocks about now.

Unperturbed, the man slid onto the stool beside her and dropped his gear bag at his feet. He gestured to the bartender, a forty-something woman dressed in a sheer black lace dress that clearly revealed her heavy, bare breasts beneath it. "I'll have a tonic with lime, please," he said. Turning back toward Allie, he smiled broadly. "Bob's the name. Master Bob to those lucky few. What's your name, pretty girl?"

"Allie," Allie replied, resisting the urge to tell the guy she wasn't interested. She had come to this party, after all. It wasn't his fault she would rather be home watching the latest episode of *Ray Donovan*. She managed a return smile.

The bartender set Bob's drink on the bar, took his money and turned away. Bob glanced furtively around the room, then reached into his bag and pulled out a small silver flask. He unscrewed the lid and brought his cup below bar level. With quick efficiency, he poured a healthy amount into the tonic.

Still keeping the flask below the bar, he held it out in Allie's direction. "Want to add a little zip to that OJ? Tanqueray gin."

Allie started automatically to refuse, but then hesitated. She had already decided she wasn't in the mood to hook up with anyone tonight, and one drink wouldn't hurt while she waited for Lauren to finish her scene. "Sure." She brought her cup below the bar. "Thanks."

Bob poured a few jiggers of the liquor into her cup, resealed the flask and slipped it back into his bag. He lifted his plastic cup in the air. "Cheers."

They touched cups and each took a swallow. The orange juice now packed a powerful punch and was, Allie had to admit, a definite improvement. She took another swallow. "Thanks."

Bob nodded. "No problem." He swiveled his stool so he was facing her. "So, tell me, Allie. You been in the scene long?"

"A couple of years," Allie said noncommittally. "How about you?"

Bob sat straighter and puffed out his chest. "Twenty-five plus. I'm a very experienced Dom. I have my own fully equipped dungeon in my basement."

"Impressive," Allie replied, stifling a yawn.

Bob nodded, his expression suddenly eager. "Want to blow this Popsicle stand and come see? I sense you're a submissive. I don't see a collar, so I'm assuming you're footloose and fancy free. I'd dearly love to send you flying. No strings, no sex unless you want it. What do you say?"

Allie had to laugh as she shook her head. "You don't waste any time, huh, Bob? You just cut right to the chase."

"I believe in being direct. Life's short, you know? No time like the present. Seize the day. All that good stuff. So?" He touched her arm. His fingers were damp.

She resisted the urge to pull away, not wanting to hurt the guy's feelings. "I'm sorry. I'm with someone. They're engaged in a scene right now, but we came together. Maybe another time, Bob."

She'd left the gender of whom she was with purposely vague, hoping Bob would assume it was a guy. It appeared he did, because he frowned and said, "What kind of idiot would leave a hot girl like you at the bar while he scened with someone else?"

When Allie didn't reply, he added, "Okay, fine. Let's you and me go into a private scene room then, okay?" He hoisted his gear bag onto his lap. "What are you into? Whipping? Candle wax? Doctor/patient role-play? Whatever you want, babe, I'll give it to you. Master Bob will make all your fantasies come true."

She had to give the guy an A for effort. She shouldn't have let Lauren talk her into this. She needed to learn to say *no*. She would start practicing right now. "I'm sorry, Bob. Not tonight."

Bob blew out a breath, reached for his gin and tonic and downed the remainder of it in one long gulp. "Fine, fine. I get it. You're just not interested. Can't blame a guy for trying, right?"

Allie smiled. "Thanks for understanding. It's not you, it's me." God, how many times had she said *that* in her life? The sad thing was, it was true more often than not. "My head's just not in the right place tonight."

"I get it." Bob gestured toward the bartender and nodded at his glass. She appeared in front of him a moment later and poured more tonic into his cup, adding a slice of lime. Once she had gone, Bob performed his operation below the bar again, pouring gin into his drink. He held out the flask toward Allie, who shook her head no.

Bob put his elbows on the bar and stared moodily into space. "You should be with a younger guy anyhow," he said, after downing nearly half of his second drink. "I'm probably old enough to be your dad. What are you, twenty-five? Twenty-six?"

"Thirty last week," Allie said, still a little stunned to realize she'd hit thirty and was still alone.

"And you're here with a guy who scenes with other women?" Bob queried, his bushy eyebrows raised.

"A girl," Allie admitted. "My friend, Lauren. She needed a ride."

"Ah, I see," Bob said. "That makes more sense, then. Though I can't for the life of me understand why someone so beautiful is unattached."

Allie smiled. "Well, thanks. I guess I just haven't found the right guy."

"The right Master," Bob said.

Allie nodded. "Yeah, that too."

"Hard to meet folks at these parties and those lame munches, am I right? You end up getting hit on by old dudes like me." Bob laughed.

Allie smiled ruefully. "It is hard. Boston's a huge city, but the BDSM community is pretty small. Pretty insular."

"Agreed. Hey, you know what you should do?" Bob turned toward her once more, his face animated.

"What's that?" Was he going to try another come-on line? God, she hoped not.

"You should try the internet."

Allie laughed. "The internet? That's the worst place to meet guys. They're all liars and scammers. Players."

"I hear ya. But I'm not talking about the free sites. I'm talking about a particular site I think would meet your needs. It's a hundred dollars for the first month, and then thirty dollars a month after that. I admit, kind of steep, but ultimately that's a good thing, because it weeds out the riff-raff, the players, you know?"

Allie opened her mouth to dismiss Bob's idea out of hand, but he stopped her with a hand over hers. "No, wait. Hear me out. It's a relatively new site, and, I don't mind admitting, it's one of my pet projects. I hired the best tech guys to make it a reality, and there's a full-time moderator to keep the place real. The site has really taken off since it went live three months ago. A young woman like you would have her pick of Doms from all over the country, I guarantee."

He pulled a small card out of his back pocket and placed it on the bar in front of Allie. It read *BDSMConnections – a discreet site for discerning individuals serious about the scene* and listed a website address. Allie glanced from the card to Bob. Had his whole spiel to this point been nothing more than a sales pitch? Still, she had to admit, the idea of a legit BDSM site appealed to her.

Allie was silent as she thought about what a hundred dollars would buy her—groceries for two weeks, part of a car payment, part of her credit card bill, which had somehow gotten away from her over the past few months. As much as she hated to admit it, a hundred bucks—maybe nothing to a guy like Bob—was a lot of money to someone like her.

She pushed the card back toward Bob. "That's a lot of money for something like that."

"Yeah, I know. I don't envy you young people, trying to make it in this world. Things were a lot easier back in my day." He reached down and pulled something out of his bag. Allie saw it was a pen, heavy and fine, like his watch. He put his hand over the card and brought it toward him. Flipping it over, he scrawled something on the other side. He pushed the card back in her direction.

"I just gave you a free access code. You'll see where to enter the information when you sign up. It will allow you to use the site free for a month, and decide if it's for you or not. No strings. You don't like it, you just let it expire. There's no automatic renewal or any of that bullshit other sites try to pull."

He swiveled his stool away from the bar and stood, pulling his too-small vest down over his belly. He turned to Allie with a smile and extended his hand, which she took automatically.

"It was nice to meet you, Allie. I wish you all the luck in the world. My sign-on at the site is Master underscore Bob." He grinned, dropping her hand. "Yeah, I know. Real original, right? But it gets the message across. Keep it simple, I always say. I hope I'll see you at BDSMConnections. Now, if you'll excuse me, I see a lovely lady sitting alone at that table over there." Grabbing his gear bag from the floor, he tipped a nonexistent hat and walked away.

Allie turned back to the bar and looked again at the card. She closed her hand over it, smiled and shrugged. Why not?

~*~

Liam Byrne opened the link for BDSMConnections and scrolled through the new female members. He still couldn't quite believe he was bothering, but reminded himself it was just for fun. No expectations, no emotional investment, no big deal. Just reaching out into the void to see what he might find.

The place did seem to attract a higher quality of clientele than the usual BDSM hookup sites, so many of which were just fronts for escort services and players. A photo was required, as well as a detailed profile. No random shots of disembodied genitalia were permitted. In the month he'd been on the site, he'd made a few nice connections, had a number of mildly stimulating sex chats and exchanged some thought provoking emails with women who had potential, if and when he ever decided he was ready to meet them face-to-face. If nothing else, the site had provided a few hours of pleasant distraction, of getting out of his own head. That was certainly worth something.

He clicked on a photo that caught his eye—a decent quality headshot of an attractive thirty-something woman. She was very pretty, with long, blond hair cut nicely around an oval face, her dark eyes and complexion probably an indication that blond wasn't her natural color.

Then he read her profile tag line: *BrattySexKitten – I've been a very bad girl. I need a strong Master to put me in my place.* He shook his head. No thank you. Not his style. He wasn't interested in playful slap and tickle as a form of foreplay. He wanted more. He *needed* more.

When he found the right woman, she would kneel before him and offer herself completely, without reservation. The connection had to be real. It had to be a true exchange of power. She would give him the gift of her total sensual submission, and he, in return, would cherish and nurture that gift.

Liam grinned at himself and shook his head. He could almost hear Matt's chuckle. *"Dude, you're not going to find the love of your life on some hookup site, no matter how pricey the monthly fee. You've got to* get out *there, man. You've got to take risks. Life isn't a dress rehearsal. This is all we got. You, of all people, should know it can be snatched away at any moment."*

"Yeah, yeah," Liam said aloud, as if Matt were actually beside him. Absently, he leaned down to massage the pain in his left leg as he scanned the screen for something more promising.

Then he saw her.

He stared for a long time at the image of a young woman with a tumble of coppery hair that fell around her shoulders. She had sparkling blue eyes and a cute little nose, but it was the smile that drew him in and held him fast.

It wasn't just the beautiful, sensual line of her pouty lips lifting up to reveal white, even teeth, or the deep dimple in her left cheek. For the first time in his life, he understood on a gut level what people meant when they said a smile lit up an entire face. She radiated a kind of innocent joy, coupled with saucy sweetness. Yet, in those deep, sky-blue eyes, he also saw shyness, or maybe it was sadness? Whatever it was, the combination of emotions playing over her lovely face worked somehow to make his stomach flip and his heart ache.

He held his breath as he read her tag line. *Sub Allie - seeking intensity of experience with an experienced, honest Dom who understands the power and grace of total sensual submission.*

Holy shit.

He clicked on the icon that allowed him access to her profile. He was able to view the number of people who had already contacted her since she'd signed up two days before. Shit—forty-seven guys had already poked, winked at and/or emailed her. Should he even bother?

He knew even as the question floated through his mind that of course he would bother. He would get in line with the rest of them and beg for a chance to say hi. Jesus, was he pathetic or what?

Stop it. You're just exploring. Reaching out. Remember: no expectations. No big deal.

She was two years younger than he and single. She was from Massachusetts—the other side of the country. That was okay—it wasn't like he planned to meet her in real life any time soon. She had extensive experience in the scene—that was good. Liam wasn't up for training a virgin sub. Been there, done that.

He scanned the checklist of desires and turn-offs. She had checked off virtually every category of BDSM play, including bondage, erotic torture, sensory deprivation, whipping, spanking, and even needle, knife and blood play. Under the category of *hard limits* she had written: *no scat, no bestiality, no children. Other than that, I trust my Master to take me where I need to go.*

Was she real?

Liam's cock hardened as he imagined Allie—a terrific name that perfectly matched that smile—bound and suspended from the beams in his dungeon basement, her naked body slowly spinning as he caressed her flesh with a whip and painted dark red welts across her skin.

He pulled the keyboard closer and positioned his fingers over the keys.

From: Liam B.

To: Sub Allie

Subject: Your profile

Hi Allie,

I saw your profile and wanted to introduce myself. My name is Liam Byrne. I am thirty-two and single, never married. I am sexually dominant with a passion for all things BDSM. I, too, have had extensive experience in the lifestyle. I have lived with two different women also into the scene, and while the BDSM connection with each was intense and satisfying as far as it went, the relationships eventually ran their course and we parted ways.

Liam paused and reread what he wrote. Too much information? It sounded like he couldn't sustain a relationship; like he'd been dumped. Which was actually true, at least with Lila, though she hadn't left him because he wasn't a good Dom. She left him because— *Stop. You don't dwell on that shit, remember? The past is the past.*

He deleted what he'd written and started again.

Hi Allie,

I was struck by the poetry and passion of your profile. It is refreshing to discover a kindred spirit. I hope you will take the time to read my profile to determine if you agree there is potential between us. I look forward to hearing from you.

Regards, Liam

He stared at what he'd written and nodded, satisfied. Short and sweet. If she was interested enough to click on his profile link, she'd learn what she needed to know about his status, likes and dislikes. The headshot was from before the accident, but he still looked the same, if perhaps a little less carefree and clueless.

"Just do it," he said aloud. "Nothing ventured, nothing gained. Hit the fucking send button."

He did.

Chapter 2

Allie's laptop pinged, the sound indicating another email. She looked up from her worktable, which was strewn with gold and silver wire, stones, precious gems and strips of raw silk.

Though she'd been skeptical at first, she'd used the access code the guy at Spanked had given her and signed up the next morning. After all, it wasn't like she was meeting Master Right on her own. Maybe widening the selection pool to include online possibilities made sense, if she wanted to meet someone before the decade was out.

She had to admit, as far as that sort of site went, BDSMConnections was a pretty good one. At least you weren't barraged with constant, pulsing ads of naked, impossibly endowed bleached blondes on their hands and knees making that odd face they made that was half-pout, half-grimace, which Allie supposed men must find sexy, but she sure didn't.

Everyone on the site was required to complete a detailed questionnaire about who they were and what they were looking for, and include a headshot. No photos of some old guy's bare, saggy ass in a thong or a close-up of an erect penis and balls were permitted, thank goodness. Those, she supposed, would come later in private emails. Gosh, she couldn't wait.

Don't be cynical, she could hear Lauren saying.

Almost the second she'd filled out her profile and posted her picture, she'd been inundated with emails from guys asking for everything from a private sex chat quickie to an offer to fly her, all expenses paid, to Dubai to serve as the personal sex slave of some supposed prince or other. Uh, thanks but no thanks.

Still, the site was fun to navigate. You could view everyone's complete profile, and there was a thumbnail headshot attached to every email so you could put a face with a name. The place had several thousand members from all over the country. Who knew, maybe Mr. Right was just waiting for Allie to find him.

Some of the guys were a little too sadistic, even for her taste. While she fantasized about being suspended and whipped until she orgasmed from the erotic pain, one guy, styling himself as Marquis de Cruel, wanted to take it a step further, whipping her until she passed out in a pool of her own blood. Marquis de Criminally Insane might have been a better user name, though she did understand fantasy did not necessarily equal reality. In this case, she fervently hoped not.

No question though, the place was a definite time sucker. It was ridiculously easy to spend way too much time scrolling through the profiles of potential lovers, and time wasn't something she managed all that well in the first place. Though she had the *luxury* of being her own boss, that came with the *stress* of being her own boss. If she didn't produce, she didn't eat. It was that simple. Though it was going on ten at night, she still had several pieces left to complete by tomorrow, and no Rumpelstiltskin was going to appear to do it for her. On top of this job, she had three new necklace commissions to fill, plus the show coming up for that new boutique in Cambridge. She had no business checking emails.

Ping.

"Okay, okay," Allie said aloud in the way people who live alone often do. She pushed back from the table. "I'll just take a quick break and see which prince wants to fly me to what country today."

She went over to the desk and tapped a key to wake her laptop screen. Sure enough, the email was from BDSMConnections, advising her that she had twenty-six new emails on the site. She clicked the saved icon in her bookmarks to open the site and navigated to the emails. While Allie made it a point to read all the emails eventually, since it only seemed fair to at least give them a shot if they'd gone to the trouble to contact her, now she just scrolled through the pictures to see if there was anyone there who grabbed her attention enough to merit a read right now, when she should be working.

Then she saw him.

Very dark hair cut a little long, matched by a few days' stubble over an angular face with a firm jaw and chin, a wide mouth, a slightly crooked nose and startlingly green eyes. He was very handsome. No, handsome wasn't the word, or maybe not enough of a word. Something in his expression was arresting, powerful. Dare she say it—masterful. She could feel his pull as if he were summoning her from the screen. Her knees actually tingled with a sudden desire to kneel before this man, this tiny thumbnail of a man's face, if she was to be accurate. How crazy was that?

She was momentarily distracted by several small boxes that appeared at the bottom of the screen. They were chat requests from members currently online who must have noticed she'd logged on. She ignored them, too focused on what she was doing even to hit the X button on each that would make them disappear.

Instead she clicked on the icon to open the email.

From: Liam B.

To: Sub Allie

Subject: Your profile

Allie held her breath as she scanned the email, looking for the false step, the insincere come-on, the impossible promises of instant submissive Nirvana if she just hooked up with this amazing Master. She blew out the breath when she came to the end of the short, direct and simple email.

"You passed the first test, Liam B."

She clicked on the link in his signature line that took her to his profile, reading more slowly as she perused his likes and dislikes, hard limits, turn-ons, experience in the scene and what he was looking for in a partner. The virtual pen she always kept poised in her virtual hand hovered, ready to mark a little X beside something he said, but no virtual red ink flowed. He was everything she sought in a Master— dominant, self-assured without being arrogant, heavily into the full and intense exploration of all four of those marvelous initials—B, D, S and M. It didn't hurt that he was young and single and extremely easy on the eyes.

The guy was perfect.

At least on paper.

Another small message box popped up at the bottom of her screen and Allie nearly hit the X, her finger stopping just in time as she read the name at the top of the box: Liam B.

He was online!

Ridiculously, her finger actually shook as she pressed the key to activate the private message chat.

Liam B.: Hi there. I see you were checking out my profile. Did I pass the test?

Allie was grinning so hard her cheeks hurt.

Sub Allie: Actually, yes. With flying colors.

Liam B.: Very cool. You passed mine as well.

That took her a little aback. So men had tests too? Well, of course they must, at least discerning men, which Liam B. obviously was. Little undulating bubbles appeared on the small chat screen, indicating he was typing. Allie waited for the next message to appear.

Liam B.: Thing is, I don't know about you, but I hate internet chatting. Would you be amenable to a quick phone call if it's not too late on your side of the country?

Your side of the country.

Shit! She'd been so caught up reading his answers to the BDSM questions, she hadn't noticed where he was from. She glanced again at the profile, clicking the section with geographic information. Her heart sank when she read he lived in Portland, Oregon. Only a billion miles across the continent.

Allie sighed aloud.

The message bubbles appeared again.

Liam B.: If not, it's cool. But if you're up for it, that would be great. I think it's a more authentic way to connect—to cut to the chase, if you will. I just want to say hi.

Allie thought about it. So, he was on the other side of the continent. So what? There were airplanes, right? Not that she planned to leap onto one and fly across the country any time soon. She was just in the throes of a very new infatuation. She knew nothing about this guy, this Liam B., beyond what he'd chosen to carefully craft in his profile. For all she knew he was actually five hundred pounds, bald and twice her age. Or married. Or secretly submissive. Oh, those were the worst. The ones who pretended they were Doms, but really they wanted a Dominatrix—a "strong woman"—that was usually giveaway terminology—to help them connect with their submissive side. No thank you!

A phone call was probably a really good idea. You could learn more from talking for a just a few minutes than from reading a profile checklist and a few sentences about goals and experience.

Liam B.: Hey, no big deal. Maybe another time.

"Wait!" Allie cried aloud. "Don't go!" She typed rapidly.

Sub Allie: Sorry! I hadn't realized you were in Oregon. I was just thinking about that.

Liam B.: Since we haven't even said hi yet, it might be jumping the gun a bit to worry about our respective locations. ☺

That stung, but at least he'd used the smiley emoticon.

Sub Allie: Point taken.

What the hell. Nothing ventured...

Sub Allie: Here's my cell number.

She picked up her phone and stared at it as she waited for it to ring. Within a few seconds, the chimes she'd chosen for people not in her contact list began to tinkle. Her heart racing, feeling more like fourteen than thirty, Allie swiped the screen to connect the call.

"Hello?" she said. "This is Allie."

The man spoke in a deep, pleasing baritone, a smile in his voice. "Hi, Allie. A pleasure to meet you. I'm Liam. Liam Byrne."

~*~

Liam gripped the bar and pulled himself up again. He had a nice burn going in his arms and upper back. Just another ten and he would hit the shower.

He heard the doorbell ring, the three short jabs and one long that told him who was at the door. "Come in. It's open," he called, not that he needed to. Matt Wilson had a key and would let himself in if Liam didn't appear within a minute or so.

Liam continued to lift and lower himself on the bar in his small home gym as he heard his front door open and then close. "Hey, it's me.

Where are you?"

"Back here in the gym. I'm almost done with my workout. Come on back."

Liam could hear Matt making his way through the living room. He grabbed his towel and wiped the sweat from his face and neck.

"Hey there." Matt stuck his head in the doorway. "Did you forget about the movie?"

"Sorry, I didn't realize it was so late." Liam glanced at the wall clock.

"No problem. The movie's not for another hour, and they always have all those previews."

"Okay. I need to shower and I'll be ready."

"Take your time. I know where the beer is."

When Liam entered his living room, Matt was seated on the couch, doing something on his phone. He looked up as Liam came into the room and pointed toward Liam's desk. "Okay, out with it. Who is that gorgeous babe on your laptop? Did you forget to close out the porn film you were jacking off to or is there something I need to know?"

"What are you talking about?" Even as he asked the question, Liam could feel his face heat. He moved toward the laptop and shut the lid. "What are you doing snooping around on my laptop anyway?"

"Not snooping. She was right there, smiling at me like a dimpled angel. Not my fault you don't use a screen saver, bro. Now out with it. Who is she? The fact that you're blushing tells me that's more than some random picture you stumbled across during a masturbatory expedition. Oh! Did you meet her on that S&M singles site you signed up for?"

"Yeah," Liam admitted. Why didn't he tell Matt all about it? He would. Of course he would. Just not yet. It was still too new, too special, to talk about it with anyone. He wasn't ready. Eager to change the subject, he said, "Did you already get the movie tickets online?"

Matt grinned. "Okay, okay. We can talk about it—about her—later. I'm glad you're starting to get back into the game, my friend. It's been long enough. It's time to move forward."

Not comfortable with the direction of the conversation, Liam again steered it to their night out. "Assigned seats?" he queried.

"Yep. I know you like the aisle in the row closest to the exit door. It's all taken care of."

Liam smiled and relaxed. "Thanks, buddy. What would I do without you?"

"What indeed?" Matt retorted with a wry grin. "I often ask myself that very question."

After the movie, over pizza and beer at Pinky's, Matt said, "So, now that you've had time to regroup, tell me more about the babe in the bikini on the beach. Is she an actual sub, or some wannabe who read *Fifty Shades* with her book club?"

Liam laughed in spite of himself. "Allie seems like the real thing. But you know"—he looked down at his beer mug, afraid his face might give away the sudden, powerful rush just saying her name caused—"it's not like I'm actually looking to meet someone in person. Going on these sites, it's something to do. Something to pass the time."

Matt shook his head, a wry smile on his face. "Oh, yeah? Is that why you're turning beet red and mumbling down into your beer like a teenager?"

Liam lifted his head. "What? I have no idea what you're talking about," he lied. "We exchanged a few emails and I've talked to her a few times on the phone, that's all. Shit, she lives across the country. It's not like I plan to hook up with her or anything. I mean, hell"—his indignation was real now, though it wasn't directed at Matt—"why would a girl like that want to hook up with a guy like me?"

Matt placed his hand on Liam's arm, his voice gentle. "Why wouldn't she, Liam? Any sub would be incredibly lucky to have you as a Master. Just ask Bonnie. She talked about the scene you did with us last year for like a month afterward. I had to threaten to gag her if she didn't shut up about it already." He barked a laugh. "Shit, if I weren't completely secure as her Dom, and if you weren't my best friend, I might have even been a little jealous."

Liam offered a wan smile. "Bonnie is different. And anyway, like you said, that was last year. Before"—he waved toward his legs beneath the table, a scowl moving over his face—"before this."

Matt nodded. "Yeah, I know." He took a swallow of beer and set down his mug. "Listen, Liam, I think it's great you're going online. It's a good start, and I'm proud of you. Look, I've known you a long time. Now, I may be off-base, but I'm getting the sense this girl, this Allie, is something more than a sex chat buddy, however much you're trying to downplay it. Am I right?"

Liam shook his head, though he couldn't help the smile that edged its way onto his lips. He should have known better than to think he could hide anything from Matt. "I think she might be, at that," he finally admitted. "Her name is Allie. Allie Swift." Just saying her name made him happy. "She actually reminds me a little of Bonnie, if you want to know the truth," he added. "She's smart and funny, with just the right amount of sass. She's independent and strong-willed. More important, she's genuine. I think that's what really drew me to her. "

"Sounds fantastic," Matt enthused approvingly. "And she's gorgeous, to boot. That doesn't hurt, huh?" He grinned.

Liam grinned back, though in fact it did hurt, at least when he faced the reality that they'd probably never really get together. He shook away the feeling, suddenly eager to tell his friend more about this amazing woman.

"She says she isn't interested in a 24/7 Master-slave kind of thing. You know, the way Lila *thought* she was, but she really wasn't, and the way I tried to give her what she asked for, but I really couldn't."

Matt nodded and laughed. "I remember. You had definite reservations about the whole full-immersion slave thing, but you wanted to please her. I don't know too many folks in the scene who can sustain that kind of intense relationship for more than a day or two. It takes a very particular kind of hardwiring to handle complete abdication of all self-will by one of the partners—being told when you can pee, when you can sleep, what you can wear, who you can talk to, that kind of thing. It's definitely not for most people, even if they think at first it might be."

"Yeah," Liam agreed. "Allie isn't seeking a slave experience, but she's definitely a sub, no question in my mind. She's deeply masochistic and longing to explore the kind of intensity of experience that would push past all her current boundaries. She wants to find out what she can handle—how far she can go with the right man—the right Master."

Liam looked down again, suddenly embarrassed at how much he was divulging. Saying all this aloud, even just saying her name to another person, made it suddenly more real. Still, he couldn't resist adding, "We talked about our shared desire for an erotic exchange of power; a consensual but boundary-pushing D/s relationship."

Liam paused, longing as sharp as a knife in his gut. "I *need* that, Matt." His voice cracked. He blew out a breath, forcing himself to regain control. "I want what you and Bonnie have. I want that for myself."

"And you deserve it, Liam. If anyone does, you do." Matt raised his beer mug in a salute. "So, good for you, buddy." He flashed a grin. "Now the question is, what are you going to do about it?"

~*~

Allie sat in front of her laptop, trying not to fidget as she waited for the FaceTime call. Liam had told her to dress as she normally would. He would direct her once they connected. The whole idea of an online video scene made her stomach clench, but when Liam had suggested it, she'd instantly agreed.

Allie had never gone in for online sex chatting or even phone sex. Admittedly, a face-to-face video scene was more personal and real than interacting with a disembodied voice. And, while Liam had sent her a few more pictures of himself over the past week that they'd been talking, she couldn't wait to see him on the screen, live and in person. Well, sort of in person, or as close as possible at this point.

At the stroke of ten, their agreed upon call time, the little FaceTime box appeared in the corner of Allie's screen. Blowing out a breath, she accepted the video call.

Oh god, he was real. And even better looking than his photos. His hair was a little shorter, his skin a little paler, but it was him, no question. He had mentioned he'd been in a serious car accident about a year before, but she couldn't see any sign of it. He looked pretty damn hot from where she was sitting, with a strong, sexy neck and broad shoulders. He was wearing a white, button-down shirt open at the throat to reveal a few dark curls of chest hair. She wanted to see more, more, more. He looked good enough to eat with a spoon. No, forget the spoon, she didn't need it. How could this hunk possibly be single?

"Hey there." Liam smiled broadly, laugh lines appearing at the corners of his very green eyes, which somehow seemed sad beneath the joy. "It's nice to see you face-to-face, Allie."

"Hi," Allie replied, at once happy and shy.

Liam sobered, his eyes boring into hers from the screen. "Are you ready to submit to me this evening?"

A zing of excited, nervous anticipation shot through Allie's core. She swallowed and nodded.

"Allie, for the duration of this chat, you will always answer any direct question. And you will address me as Sir. Is that clear?"

"Ooooh." The word was pulled from her like a breath of air whooshing from her soul. *Yes. Yes, yes, yes, this is what I was missing. What I need.* "Yes, uh, yes, Sir. It's clear. I think I'm ready to submit, Sir."

"You think?" Liam cocked an eyebrow.

Allie's face grew hot. She glanced at the small preview screen of herself in the corner of the app. Sure enough, she was blushing. Shit.

"I'm sorry," she said, focusing again on Liam's face. "I mean that I want to do this. I want to connect with you in a scene, but this whole setup, this FaceTime thing instead of real life..." She glanced again at herself and back at Liam. "It's"—she hunched her shoulders as she tried to formulate her thoughts—"I don't know, artificial."

Liam nodded. "Yeah, it is limited. But for right now it's what we've got." He regarded her a moment. "Here's what I want you to do. Turn off your preview screen so you can focus solely on me. All right?"

"Yes, Sir." Allie closed the preview screen, glad not to have to see herself.

"Good." Liam leaned back a little in his chair, allowing her a view of the lower half of his body. He was wearing faded jeans and the bulge between his legs was most alluring. Allie actually salivated at the thought of seeing his cock, and she swallowed quickly. She attempted to look serene and properly submissive, hoping the lust wasn't too obvious on her face.

"Let's review the guidelines we discussed last night," Liam continued, apparently mercifully unaware of where her eyes had been lingering. "Do you have the toys I asked you to assemble?"

Allie glanced at the tray of BDSM toys next to her laptop. "Yes, Sir."

"Show me each item and tell me its purpose."

Though Allie was no stranger to BDSM play, once again her face heated. What was it about this guy that left her slightly off kilter?

She picked up the first item and held it toward the screen. "These are the clover clamps, Sir."

"And their purpose?"

"To use on my nipples, Sir." Her nipples stiffened at her words.

Liam nodded. "That's correct. And not only your nipples, sub Allie. We might also use them on your cunt, if not this evening, one day soon."

"Oooh," Allie sighed, the word once more drawn from her without her permission or intention.

"Next item," Liam directed.

Allie picked up her much-loved leather wrist cuffs, the metal clips already attached. "These are my cuffs, Sir. For binding my wrists together."

"Excellent, sub Allie." Liam's eyes glittered. "Next item."

Allie picked up the ball gag, not her favorite toy, a gift from her last boyfriend. She held it up. "This is a ball gag, Sir. For keeping me quiet if that pleases you."

"You don't like ball gags." It was a statement. Was she that obvious?

"No, Sir. Not really."

"Why not?"

In the week they'd been talking, Allie had come to trust Liam. Though she hadn't shared everything, she had strived to be honest when talking about her feelings and desires in the scene. "I don't like the taste of the rubber ball, Sir. And I don't like the drool. And I don't like not being able to speak—to communicate if I need to say something. You know, like my safeword."

Liam nodded slowly. "I understand. Unfortunately, or fortunately, I suppose, depending on your perspective, as a submissive and slave, what you like or don't like isn't my first concern, though of course I will take it into consideration when deciding what is best for you, and what best serves me. You do understand that, don't you, sub Allie?"

"Yes, Sir," Allie whispered, something clicking into place inside her soul. *He gets it.* "Thank you, Sir."

"You're welcome. Now. It's time. I remember your safeword is diamond, but you won't have need of it today. This is just an exploration, really. A test of your obedience and sexual responsiveness." Allie's mouth went suddenly dry, her pussy instantly wet. "First, push your chair back from the screen and stand up so I can see your entire body."

Allie did as she was told.

Liam regarded her intently, his eyes sweeping her form as if he could already see her naked beneath her top and jeans. Her nipples jutted against the lace of her bra and the silk of her tank top. Her heart thudded against her ribcage.

"Take off your jeans."

Allie kicked off her sandals and unzipped her jeans. She was glad she hadn't chosen the skin-tight ones, which she had to do a kind of chicken dance to get out of. These, while form fitting, were loose enough to let slide gracefully down her legs. She stood tall once more, now just in panties and her top, struggling to remain calm and composed.

"Now your top and your bra."

Okay, no big deal. She'd stripped at the play clubs in front of strangers, though in that kind of atmosphere, nudity was more the norm than the exception. She had a decent body, even if her breasts weren't quite as large as she'd like, her butt a little bigger than she'd wish. She could totally do this. Piece of cake.

"Now the panties."

Okay. No problem. The Brazilian wax she'd had two days ago, which had hurt like a motherfucker and not in the good way, had been worth it. She was smooth as a baby. She tugged at the bit of silk that covered her mons and kicked away the panties. Resolutely, heart pounding, she faced the screen.

"Lift your arms and lace your fingers behind your neck. Spread your legs to shoulder-width apart and remain silent and at attention until I tell you to move."

Biting her lip, Allie assumed the standard at-attention pose. Judging by the bulge that had grown substantially in his jeans, Sir Liam liked what he saw. She shifted her gaze to his face. His eyes were hooded with lust, his tongue moving sensually over his lower lip. "Turn around slowly," he said softly. "I want to see your ass."

Allie turned, feeling especially vulnerable with her backside to the screen, naked and alone in her small apartment. After several beats, Sir Liam said, "You may turn around again." Once she had done so, he said, "You please me, sub Allie. Are you ready to continue?"

"Yes, Sir Liam," Allie said in a low voice.

"I like that. Sir Liam." He smiled. Allie ached to kiss that lush, sensual mouth. "You may lower your arms now. I want you to stimulate your nipples until they are fully erect."

Allie dropped her arms and reached for her breasts. Her nipples were already hard as little stones, but she obediently rolled them between forefingers and thumbs.

"Good. Now, put the clover clamps in place, one on each nipple. Make sure to go all the way back to the base of the nipple."

Allie knew very well how to apply the clamps for maximum hold, but she wasn't about to lecture her new Dom. She quietly reached for the clamps. Pulling her right nipple taut with one hand, she opened the clamp with the other and let it close over the nipple.

She blew out an audible breath as the pain registered along her nerve endings and ricocheted through her brain. Reaching for the second nipple, she clamped it in the same fashion, blowing out another breath as she focused on harnessing and assimilating the erotic pain now throbbing at both nipples.

Beautiful," Sir Liam breathed from the screen. He had leaned forward, his gaze fixed on her with a fierce intensity. "Sit down on the chair and spread your legs. Show me your cunt."

Allie, whose legs had grown a little wobbly during the nipple clamping, was glad to sit down, but not thrilled at Sir Liam's latest directive. She had never been comfortable exposing herself in this way, and hated direct scrutiny of her private parts. Still, she didn't want to blow it now, not her first time in a scene with this impossibly sexy Dom. Scooting slightly forward on the chair, she forced her legs to part.

"Wider. Show me your cunt." The command in his voice made it somehow easier to obey. Allie tried not to focus on the tingling, painful throb of her nipples. She spread her legs wider and tilted her pelvis slightly to offer Sir Liam a better view. She closed her eyes as the heat once more washed over her face and neck.

"Jesus, you're lovely," he whispered with sweet, aching conviction. Allie opened her eyes, confused to see the longing and pain in his face. But as quickly as it was there, it was gone, the masterful Sir Liam once more in full control.

"Place the cuffs on your wrists and clip them together."

Allie did so, loving, as she always did, the feel of the soft, well-worn leather against her skin. With some twisting and maneuvering, she managed to hook the two clips so her wrists were bound together in front of her. She looked up at the screen, where Sir Liam was watching intently, his hand now covering his crotch.

"You are beautiful, sub Allie," he said, his voice low and masterful. "Now you're going to masturbate for me with those shackled hands. I want to watch you come."

Allie's heart sank, just a little. She hated masturbating in front of someone else, even a lover. But maybe it would be different with Sir Liam. Maybe, this time, she wouldn't have to pretend.

She licked the fingers of her right hand and lowered her bound wrists, glad at least to partially conceal her spread pussy with her hands. Her nipples had numbed to a manageable throb, which beat in time to the pulse in her rock-hard clit. She needn't have licked her fingers—she was soppingly, embarrassingly wet.

She let her eyes close as she began to swirl her fingers over her labia, spreading her natural lubricant into the soft folds. She moaned softly as she settled into a good rhythm. She could do this. She could so do this. Sexy, sensitive, dominant Sir Liam was watching her, a witness to her lust. She would pretend he was the one touching her. She would imagine he was twisting her nipples. She could almost feel the grip of his strong, sure hand around her throat, holding her down in a primeval show of dominance and control. She shuddered as she visualized his whip, a cat with knotted ends that left tiny welts with each delicious, searing stroke.

Ah, she was close. She was close! Maybe, just maybe, this time—

"Open your eyes. Focus on my face. I will tell you when you have permission to climax."

Startled by his voice, Allie opened her eyes to focus on the man she'd been conjuring so vividly in her imagination. He had shifted slightly in his seat, and she could no longer see the lower half of his body, but she guessed from the way his right upper arm was moving that he was masturbating, too. No fair—she wanted to see.

She knew better than to ask, however. Sir Liam wanted her to focus on his face while she made herself come.

You can do it, you can do it. Come on! She rubbed furiously, sliding a finger inside as she stroked her sensitive clit with increasing abandon. She began to pant, her heart beating wildly, sweat breaking on her brow.

"That's it, yes!" Sir Liam panted in return. "Yes, yes. Oh! Now! Come for me, sub Allie. Now."

She tried. Oh, how she tried, desperate to catch and ride that wave for Sir Liam, for herself. But the harder she reached for it, the more it receded. She could hear from Sir Liam's voice and see from the twisted, ecstatic expression on his handsome face that he was climaxing at that moment.

I can't disappoint him. I have to please him. I want to please him, more than I've ever wanted to please anyone. Damn it, Allie, just do it!

Meg Ryan took over, channeling her very best *When Harry Met Sally* impression at Katz's Deli through Allie's psyche. When she'd finished moaning, arching and sighing, even she was almost convinced she'd come.

Shaking back her hair, she sat up in the chair and focused on the screen. Sir Liam was smiling broadly once more, the unmistakable look of male pride at having satisfied his woman on his face. "You please me, sub Allie."

Allie smiled back, ignoring the small, niggling voice of her conscience. "Thank you, Sir," she replied.

Chapter 3

Liam sat bolt upright in bed, his heart pounding so hard it felt as if it had burst through his chest. He was panting, his body bathed in sweat, his leg throbbing as if newly mangled. His own shout had woken him, the sound still reverberating in his brain. The oncoming car hurtling out of control still loomed large and terrifying in his mind's eye, as if the image had been burned onto his retinas.

Your fault, your fault, your fault.

He reached for the bedside lamp and switched it on to rob the nightmare of its lingering power. He glanced at the clock. A little after three in the morning—still too early to get up, but there was no way he was going back to sleep for a while.

He threw back the sweat-soaked sheets and swung his legs over the side of the bed. "You're lucky," he reminded himself aloud, as he often did when the pain licked like fire through the muscle, tendon and bone. "At least you're still alive." He eyed the bottle of pain pills, decided the pain was manageable, and hoisted himself to his feet.

He made his way slowly toward the bathroom without the benefit of his cane. He focused on walking with a smooth, steady gait, but was too tired to manage it. He turned on the shower and stood under the steamy spray for several minutes, letting the warmth soothe and settle him. Then he soaped up, rinsed, turned off the water and grabbed a towel.

He dried himself, wrapped the damp towel around his waist and went to the kitchen where he got a glass of water from the tap and drank it all. He felt calm and refreshed now, but also fully awake. Maybe a chapter or two of the book he was reading would lull him back to sleep. Returning to the bedroom, he stripped the still sweat-damp sheets from the bed and quickly remade it.

Climbing between the cool, fresh sheets, he reached for the e-reader from the nightstand, but his fingers instead chose the iPad. With Allie's prior permission, he had recorded the intense, amazing session the night before, and he clicked it open now, his free hand going for his cock.

Even as his shaft rose and hardened, his heart squeezed with tender amusement at her obvious shyness, at least in the beginning. He loved her strength and her passion, but the sweet overlay of hesitation, of vulnerability, touched something at his core.

He stopped thinking as he watched her strip, her lovely, slender body coming into view on the screen. Had he been there in front of her, he would have run his fingertips lightly under her arms and over her smooth, soft mons. He would have let his fingers slip lower to caress the cleft, to feel the heat and the wetness there.

His cock throbbed as she turned in a graceful pirouette to reveal her luscious ass. He had been especially pleased to see the round, generous globes, ideal for spanking, perfect for whipping. Her legs and arms were tan compared to the creamy white of her lovely ass. As he pumped his cock, he imagined stroking her soft skin as she lay over his lap. He would start slowly, acclimating her to his touch. He would gauge her reaction to the first sharp slaps as he admired the jiggle of feminine flesh. He would slap harder, his palm cracking against her ass cheeks until she was panting and moaning. He would go as long as he could, until her white flesh was a dark, mottled red. He would continue until she began to struggle and cry in earnest. He would keep going until she surrendered; until she gave in to the erotic pain and let him guide her through it to where she needed to go.

She was touching herself now on the screen, so hot, so fucking sexy with her wrists bound together, her legs splayed, her head thrown back. Liam held himself on the edge until she was there, nearly there. *Yes, yes, come for me, Allie, come for me.*

He let the iPad fall to the bed as hot spurts of jism ribboned over his stomach. He lay motionless, eyes closed, for several long moments as his heart eased its rhythm. Finally, he opened his eyes, reached for a washcloth from the nightstand drawer, wiped himself clean and tossed the cloth onto the dirty sheets piled on the floor. With a satisfied sigh, he closed his tablet and rolled onto his side, letting his eyes close once more.

Several nights later, Liam sat at the dinner table at Matt and Bonnie's house, pleasantly full and a little tipsy from several glasses of good red wine. "That was delicious, Bonnie. Thank you." He set down his fork with a satisfied sigh.

"You want some more?" Bonnie pointed toward the half-eaten tray of lasagna. "There's plenty left."

Liam patted his full stomach. "I couldn't eat another bite."

"Too bad," Matt chimed in. "That means you don't have room for the chocolate mousse she made for dessert. Ah well, more for me."

"I didn't say that," Liam retorted with a laugh. "I couldn't eat another bite of the lasagna because I'm saving room for the mousse."

"Boys, boys"—Bonnie chuckled as she rose and began to clear the dishes—"there's plenty for everyone. You know our family motto—only too much is enough."

Liam watched as Bonnie moved gracefully around the table. Her dark hair was loose, tendrils falling over her face as she moved. She wore a silky red dress that clung to her curvaceous, lush form. Liam had always been a little in love with his best friend's wife, but he loved Matt even more, and would never, ever do anything to compromise their friendship.

Still, he did like to look, and neither Matt nor Bonnie, active in the BDSM club scene, minded a bit. In fact, it pleased Matt to show off his lovely submissive at every opportunity and she, an exhibitionist, as many subs in the club scene were, seemed happiest when naked and in chains, no matter who was present.

Bonnie disappeared into the kitchen, returning a moment later with three fluted glasses filled with dark, rich mousse topped with whipped cream. Matt, meanwhile, had moved to the liquor cabinet in the corner of the dining room. He set three brandy snifters on the table and poured several fingers of Cognac into each glass.

Liam couldn't stop the moan of pure delight as he took his first bite of Bonnie's heavenly chocolate mousse. She was watching him over the rim of her brandy glass, a small smile on her lips. Matt, too, was watching him. They exchanged a quick glance, triumph in Matt's expression, a shrug of amused defeat in Bonnie's.

Liam set down his spoon. "What?" he demanded. "Why are you both staring at me like that? Do I have chocolate on my face or something?" He lifted his napkin to his mouth.

Matt laughed. "No. I made a bet with Bonnie earlier in the evening that you wouldn't say a single word during dinner about the hot girl you're having an online affair with and, sure enough, you haven't."

"You told Bonnie about her?" Even as he asked, Liam knew it was a dumb question. Matt and Bonnie told each other everything.

"He did," Bonnie interjected with a wide smile. "And I think it's wonderful, Liam. I hope things are still moving along well between you, and you're just being discreet in not telling your very best friends about the most important thing to happen to you in a long time." The laugh in her voice and the smile on her pretty face took the sting out of her words.

Liam lifted his snifter and took a long swallow of the brandy, savoring the burn as it bloomed in his chest. "Okay, okay. What do you want to know?"

"Let's start with an easy one. What does she do for a living?"

"She designs jewelry. She makes really cool stuff. She sells her work at art shows and in galleries and boutiques all over Boston. She's branching out, too. She has her own website and everything. In fact, it just went live this week." Liam couldn't help the swell of pride as he spoke, as if Allie were actually his girl, in real life.

"Hey, that's great," Bonnie said with a smile. "So, she's self-employed, just like all of us."

"Yeah, that's right." It was true—Bonnie was a therapist with a thriving private practice, Matt was a software design consultant for the high-tech music industry and Liam had forged a very successful career for himself, obtaining multi-million dollar grants for non-profit companies.

"And things are still going well between you? The connection is authentic? She's a true sub? Not just a dabbler?"

"Yes," Liam affirmed with quiet certainty.

"So, that's all wonderful news, right? You've stepped out of your comfort zone—you've taken a risk and it's paying off. That's great, Liam. I'm so happy for you," Bonnie said, smiling brightly, as if everything were that simple.

"It all sounds so easy when you put it that way." Liam blew out an angry breath at how unfair life could be. "Look, she doesn't really know"—he paused, but then forced himself to continue—"about me. The details. About the accident."

About what I did. What I failed to do.

Bonnie put her hand over Liam's, her smile falling away. The grave empathy and understanding in her eyes made Liam feel safe, and he unclenched the fist he hadn't realized he'd made. "It wasn't your fault," she said softly, cutting directly to the heart of the matter as she so often did. "You didn't cause the accident. You aren't responsible for what happened."

Liam bit his lip to keep from shouting the truth. He gave a brusque nod.

"If she's the woman you think she is," Bonnie continued, "she'll understand. You know, you Doms ask us subs to put our complete trust in you, to trust that you'll take care of us when you take control. You have to do the same, Liam. You have to learn to trust, not only in the context of D/s, but in the context of any meaningful relationship."

"Yes, Dr. Wilson." Liam forced a laugh. "Come on, Bonnie, it's like you already have us married off. I mean, yeah, she's pretty fantastic, but look, I've only known her a few weeks, okay?"

"A few weeks is plenty of time to know your own heart, especially if there's a D/s connection. Matt and I fell in love during a single scene at a mutual friend's play party," Bonnie countered. "Has she expressed an interest in meeting you face to face?"

"Well, yeah, kind of," Liam admitted.

"There you go, then." Bonnie leaned back with a satisfied smile. "It's a no-brainer."

Liam glanced at Matt, silently willing him to tell his sub to be quiet, but Matt only nodded. "I totally agree. It's time to get off your ass, Liam, my boy. Here's what you do. Invite Allie to come see you here in Portland. I have a billion free miles from all my traveling for work and we'll never be able to use them up. Say the word, and we'll book a flight for her, first class. You know you want to."

"Guys," Liam pleaded, spreading out his hands in supplication. "Give me a break. I want to meet her, yeah. But I'm just not ready yet, okay?"

It was true. He wanted to meet Allie, to hold her, to kiss her, to claim her, more than he'd ever wanted anything in his life. But he couldn't face seeing the pity and disgust in her lovely blue eyes. He couldn't bear the thought of losing her.

To his vast relief, Matt pushed back from the table and stood. "Okay, okay, you're right. We said our piece. What you do with it is up to you. Now"—he turned his gaze to Bonnie—"I want to show Liam our new toy. Go get it and wait for us in the living room."

The mood in the room shifted palpably at Matt's words. Bonnie set down her brandy glass, her face softening and suffusing with an inner light. "Yes, Sir. Thank you, Sir," she said, her voice suddenly husky. She pushed back from the table and slipped quickly from the room.

Both carrying their snifters, Liam followed Matt into the living room, settling on a chair kitty-corner to the sofa where Matt sat. He set his walking cane beside the chair and leaned back as he sipped his brandy, eager for the show to begin

Bonnie appeared a moment later, carrying something made of black leather in her hands. She handed it to Matt, who took it and said, "Present yourself, naked and on your knees in front of me."

Bonnie stepped back and at once slipped the straps of her red dress from her shoulders. It slid down her naked body like silken water, pooling at her bare feet. Liam's cock rose in automatic response at the sight, and he shifted in his chair in an effort to hide his erection.

Bonnie lowered herself gracefully to her knees in front of her Master, her eyes fixed on his face. "Tell our guest what I had made for you by the Leather Master, sub girl," Matt commanded, making no effort to hide *his* erection, which bulged proudly at his crotch.

Bonnie turned to look at Liam, her eyes shining. "It's a spiked breast binder, Sir," she said, clearly in full sub mode.

"That's right," Matt interjected with an evil smile as he held up the bondage toy for Liam to see. "These tiny spikes on the inside of the cups make for a biting reminder of who is in control. Then, these cutouts at the center of the cups leave plenty of room for some delicious nipple torture."

"Sweet," Liam said fervently, instantly picturing Allie in Bonnie's place as the wicked-looking metal spikes pressed against the smooth, soft skin of her perfect breasts.

"Let's try it out, shall we, sub girl?" Matt said, his eyes now fixed on his wife's heavy, beautiful breasts.

"Yes, Sir," Bonnie said eagerly.

Matt stood, indicating with his chin for Bonnie to rise from her knees. She lifted her arms as he strapped the wide leather band around her torso and fitted the cutout cups over her breasts. She winced in pain and pursed her lips as he tightened the buckles that held the contraption in place, but she made no protests. Her large, dark nipples were fully erect at the center of the leather cups.

Matt stepped back, admiring his leather-bound sub girl. "Beautiful," he whispered. "Does it hurt, sweetheart?"

"Yes, Sir," Bonnie breathed.

"Good. I like to make you suffer."

"Thank you, Sir."

Liam looked away, longing washing so fiercely through him he had to bite the inside of his cheek to keep from screaming.

"Hey," Matt said, making Liam look back at the couple. Matt reached into his jeans pocket, pulled something out and tossed it in Liam's direction.

Liam automatically extended his hand to catch it, and saw he held a pair of black Japanese clover clamps. He lifted his eyebrows at Matt.

"Will you do the honors, Master Liam?" Matt said with an evil grin.

Liam pushed himself to his feet as Bonnie came to stand in front of him. He grasped her right nipple between thumb and forefinger. A jolt of sweet, painful recognition moved through his muscle memory—it had been so long since he'd touched a woman in this way.

Forcing himself to focus, Liam pressed open one of the clamps. Keeping her nipple taut, he carefully closed the lightly padded ends of the clamp over the base of her nipple, a rush of sadistic pleasure shooting through his loins as pain moved like a caress over her face. He did the same to her left nipple, another jolt of power kicking through his gut as the clamp bit into her flesh.

"Jesus god," Matt whispered, his eyes fixed on Bonnie as she stood before them. "I'm the luckiest man in the world."

"You are," Liam agreed.

Matt turned to him. "Let's do a scene. It'll be like old times. We can put Bonnie through her paces in the playroom, and you can stay over in the guest bedroom. What do you say?"

Matt hadn't consulted Bonnie, but then, in this context, he didn't need to. She would submit to whatever her Master wanted for her, as it should be. Liam was tempted, and his little head counseled that he should agree at once. But his brain, or was it his heart, had other ideas.

Regretfully, he shook his head. "Thanks, Matt. And thank you, Bonnie," he added, smiling at her. "I'm incredibly tempted, don't think I'm not. But, I know this is going to sound really weird, but it just wouldn't feel right. Not without talking to Allie first. I mean, I would want her to know, to be okay with it."

Matt raised his eyebrows so high they disappeared into his hair. "So that's how it is, huh, bro? And you're trying to run that line of bullshit that it's too soon to get together with this girl?" He chuckled. "You know what they say—actions speak louder than words. Your actions tell Bonnie and me all we need to know. Isn't that right, sub girl?"

Bonnie managed a smile, despite her tortured breasts. "It certainly is, Sir." Liam couldn't swear to it, but he thought he saw a decidedly mischievous glint in her pretty, dark eyes.

~*~

Allie glanced up from her work at the sound of an email ping. Since she'd met Liam, she'd disabled the email function on the BDSMConnections site, but with the new jewelry website she'd recently set up, she needed to be responsive to customer emails, in case there was a problem.

She rose from the worktable and walked over to her desk. Sure enough, the email had come through the website. Hopefully there was no problem. For the first week or so, the shopping cart had kept screwing up, but she'd thought that was all fixed now.

Sliding onto the chair in front of the laptop, she opened the email from someone named Bonnie Wilson.

Hi Allie,

First, I wanted to say I can't wait to receive the three pieces I ordered from your site. You are a truly talented artist and I love your work.

Allie smiled, delighted she had a new customer. She'd been surprised how quickly the pieces were selling. If things continued at this rate, she wouldn't even need to worry about placing her work in boutiques and galleries, where they took half the proceeds in exchange for giving her space.

Second, I wanted to let you know we have a friend in common. His name is Liam Byrne.

Liam Byrne! What the hell? Allie's heart began to beat faster. What was going on? Was this where she found out Liam was actually married? Was the pleasant opening of this email just the precursor to the diatribe of an enraged, wronged spouse? Steeling herself, Allie forced herself to read on.

Really, Liam is more than a friend, he's like a brother to me and my husband, Matt. We are also Master and sub—Matt owns me in all the best possible ways. Liam has always been there for us, and we want to be there for him, too. Matt knows I'm writing to you, and I have his full support. Liam, however, doesn't know.

Okay, phew. No wronged spouse. But what was going on? Why was this woman emailing her? Had something happened to Liam? Allie's gut tightened in panic and she had to force herself to read on.

Liam has told us about you. You should see his face when he talks about you—it's like someone lit a candle inside his head. He just glows. I'll just tell you, girl-to-girl and sub-to-sub, the guy is head over heels crazy for you.

Allie grinned widely as she read this. Liam had talked about her! It was one thing for girlfriends to confide in each other, as she had with Lauren, but for a guy to do it, it had to be serious.

I know you two have been chatting and emailing for a few weeks now, and you're probably wondering why Liam hasn't arranged to meet you yet. As I think he told you, Liam was in a car accident about a year ago. While his physical recovery is going well enough, he's had a rough time emotionally. I hope I'm not overstepping in telling you that he was engaged to a girl who couldn't deal with the fallout from the accident.

Whoa. Allie's heart constricted with pity, followed quickly by a rising indignation. What kind of woman dumped the man she loved when he needed her most? Now that she thought about it, Liam had vaguely indicated he'd been engaged to someone a while back, but he'd never given any details about why they had broken up. To be fair, Allie hadn't volunteered too much about her failed love life either. They'd both been too busy living in the moment, she supposed, to dwell on past history.

Because of that, and some of the issues he's had to deal with in recovering from his injuries, Liam is kind of gun shy when it comes to getting involved again. To put it simply, he's dying to meet you, but he's afraid of your reaction when you see he isn't "perfect," at least as he defines it.

What I'm working up to here, Allie, is that, if you want to meet Liam and move your relationship forward, you're going to have to be the one to take the next step. That said, I can only imagine, as an independent artist making it on her own, that money doesn't grow on trees and it might not be that easy or economical for you to just book a flight from Boston to Portland.

The good news is, my husband's job requires him to travel. We have so many free miles built up we'll never be able to use them all. It would cost us nothing to get an airline ticket for you. His points work for hotels, too, and we could get you a room for however long you need. We could make the return portion of the flight open-ended so there's no pressure, no worries if things don't work out.

I'm assuming you can do your jewelry design work anywhere, or maybe you've earned a break for a week or two? The good thing about being your own boss is you're the one who approves the vacation days, right? Ha ha.

Anyway, once you got here, we could either arrange for you to meet Liam at our house for dinner, say, or (and this is my personal favorite, but bear in mind that I love romance novels, so I'm a sucker for this kind of thing) you could just show up at his door (naked and on your knees would be ideal, right? But then, we do live in a vanilla world...).

I hope you forgive and understand this invasion of your privacy. I only take this step because we love Liam, and he's literally come alive again since he found you. He's a good man and a fabulous Dom. Like my Matt, he's one of those delicious sadists with a heart of pure gold. I know I'm suggesting something pretty radical here, but that's what it might take to penetrate his defenses. And, after all, what's life without a dash of risk?

I look forward to hearing from you. You can email or call. See all my *contact info in my signature line.*

Love, Bonnie

Allie sat for several long moments staring at the screen, stunned by what she'd read. She read it a second time, savoring the sweet bits, mulling over the vague language regarding the accident and Liam's injuries, which still affected him a full year after the fact.

It must have been a pretty serious accident, and yet Allie hadn't seen any evidence during their FaceTime chats, though she had never seen him naked. She had accepted this in light of their Dom/sub connection, but now she had to wonder. What lay beneath that white button-down and those faded jeans?

She had to admire Bonnie Wilson's nerve, just writing to her out of the blue as she had done, with a complete proposal, airline tickets and all. What would Lauren think about all this? Lauren, who had been asking lately the same question Bonnie had just posed: When are you going to meet this *Über*-Dom, this sensitive, sexy, too-good-to-be-true dreamboat?

Allie grabbed her cell phone. She returned to her laptop as the call connected and Lauren picked up.

"That you, girlfriend?"

"Yeah. You have time to talk?"

"Sure. What's up?"

"You'll never guess what a crazy email I just got. I'm going to forward it to you, okay? Just stay on the line while you read it, and then tell me what you think."

"Sounds very mysterious. What's going on?"

"Just wait. It should be there. I sent it to your personal email."

"Okay." After several beats of silence, Lauren said, "Got it."

She began to laugh as she read the email, making the same assumptions and deductions aloud that Allie had when she'd first read it. "Holy shit, Allie, this *is* like a freakin' romance novel. You're going to do it, right? I mean, come on, you *have* to. Let's move it from romance novel to *erotic* romance novel. I totally agree with Bonnie. You should show up at his door, naked and on your knees."

Allie laughed. "I'm sure that would make a great first impression with his neighbors."

"So, who cares? Like Bonnie said, what's life without a little risk?"

"Yeah, but Lauren," Allie protested. "I've never done anything even remotely like this. It goes beyond risky. It's crazy!"

"Hey, crazy isn't always a bad thing. You're thirty years old and you've never been in love. So, something has to change. If you want something you've never had, you have to do something you've never done. This is clearly a gift from the universe. Accept it. Go for it."

When they hung up, Allie opened the email once more, and added Bonnie's information into her contacts. Lauren was right. This was her chance at something real, at last. She opened her contacts on her phone and scrolled down to the one that read: *Bonnie Wilson*. She closed her eyes, blew out a breath, opened them again and touched the phone number.

CHAPTER 4

Liam, his solitary dinner completed, swirled the last bit of his wine and drained the glass. He was trying to decide if he wanted a second glass of wine to take into the living room with him when the doorbell rang.

Wondering who it could be, Liam hoisted himself up from the chair, grabbed his cane and moved quickly through the house toward the door. He leaned to the peephole and peered through. The cane clattered to the floor, but he barely noticed, his heart lurching and twisting in his chest.

What the hell? Was he drunker than he thought? Was he hallucinating? He stared for several long seconds as his mind struggled to process the impossible. It was Allie, all right. She was even lovelier in real life, though he could see from her expression she was more than a little nervous.

She was standing back far enough that he could see she was wearing some kind of raincoat, buttoned to her throat, even though the evening sky was clear. Her legs were bare, a pair of pretty red high heels on her feet.

Open the door, stupid, his brain ordered. With fumbling hands, he hurried to comply. She hadn't vanished into a hallucinatory haze—there she stood, his dream girl, his sub girl, his Allie, in the flesh.

Surprise," she said, flashing a dimpled grin. "I just happened to be in the neighborhood, so…"

"Allie," Liam whispered. "You're here."

He stepped over the threshold and took her into his arms. He could smell the faint scent of her perfume, a fresh, pleasing hint of lavender. Her breath was sweet, like peppermint, and her lips were soft and yielding to his. As he kissed her, he stepped backward into the house, drawing her with him. Once inside, he pushed the door closed and pressed her against it, unable to take his mouth from hers.

When he finally pulled away, she was breathless, her eyes shining. She reached for the top button of her raincoat and opened it. Her eyes remained fixed on his as her fingers moved nimbly down the column of buttons.

When the coat fell open, Liam sucked in his breath as he stared at her naked body beneath it. She let the coat fall from her shoulders and stood proud in front of him, a vision of pure, radiant submission.

As he stared, she sank to her knees. "I'm here to offer myself to you, Sir Liam. Please accept my submission."

The Dom in Liam responded in kind, pushing away any lingering hesitation or confusion. He placed his hand lightly on her silky head. "Yes. Yes, sub Allie. I accept what you offer. Stand up, I have to kiss you again."

Allie rose and Liam took her in his arms once more, pulling her close. He kissed her lips, her eyes, her forehead, the curve of her throat. Dipping his head, he ran his tongue down her throat to her breasts. He licked her nipples, one at a time, savoring the sweet, silky hardness as she sighed her approval, her head back, her eyes closed.

When he eventually stepped back, Allie opened her eyes and blinked several times, as if awakening from a dream.

"Hi," she said with a shy laugh.

"Hi," Liam replied, grinning. "I can't believe you're here. You're supposed to be in Boston. How did you even know where I live?"

Allie wrapped her arms protectively around her torso. "Bonnie told me."

"Bonnie?" Liam echoed stupidly. "My Bonnie? Bonnie Wilson?"

"She's not yours," Allie said with an impish grin. "I'm yours. And yes, that Bonnie. Your friends, Matt and Bonnie, decided we needed to meet, and they took matters into their own hands. They sent me a ticket. I only arrived at Portland International about an hour ago."

"My friends, the matchmakers." Liam laughed, shaking his head, not sure yet if he should be furious at their meddling or eternally grateful. "You'll have to tell me the whole story, but there's time for that later. Can I get you something to drink? Do you need anything?"

Allie smiled and shook her head. "I'm fine. I freshened up at the hotel before I came over." She looked down. "I hope it's okay I'm here, Liam. Bonnie said you really wanted to see me, but were a little shy…" She trailed off, looking suddenly quite shy and vulnerable herself. Liam could only imagine the courage it had taken to fly across the country and present herself to him as she had.

He placed his hands on Allie's shoulders, staring with undisguised wonderment at her lovely face. "Trust me, Allie, it's more than okay. I'm so glad you're actually here. Thank you for doing what I couldn't." He stopped, embarrassed.

"Um…" Allie said.

"Yes, what?" Liam asked, regarding her quizzically.

"There's something I really want to do, Sir. It might be kind of, uh, un-submissive to ask but…" She trailed off, a look of uncertainty moving over her face.

"Go on," he urged, wildly curious now. "What is it?"

Allie sank once more to her knees and whispered something he couldn't quite hear.

"What?" he said. He reached down and put his finger under her chin, forcing her to look up at him. "Speak louder. I couldn't hear you."

A pretty blush moved over her face as she said, "I want to suck your cock, please, Sir. I've thought about it forever."

Liam certainly didn't need to be asked twice. He tugged at his fly, pulling it free of the row of metal buttons that held it closed. He pushed his jeans and underwear to the top of his thighs, shifting his stance to keep them in place. Sweet, sexy Allie actually licked her lips as she regarded his cock. Liam grinned, delighted. "Please me, sub Allie. Worship my cock and balls until I tell you to stop."

"Yes, Sir, thank you, Sir." Allie leaned forward to close her mouth over the head of his shaft while her long, cool fingers cupped and stroked his balls. Liam groaned with pleasure. It had been so long, he'd almost forgotten the hot, velvety caress of someone's tongue and lips on his cock. He watched as she moved forward, taking the length of him fully into her mouth, not stopping until the head of his shaft made contact with the soft flesh at the back of her throat.

He held her in place for several long beats. She didn't struggle or try to pull away, though he was reasonably sure she was unable to breathe.

"Good," he said softly. "Very good, sub Allie. You please me." The full weight of his dominant persona had settled over him now. It felt good to be back, as if he were finally fully himself again. More than good, it felt *right*.

He kept her that way several beats longer, holding his own breath to make sure he didn't overdo it. Finally, he released his hand from her head. Allie pulled back and drew in a quick, deep breath. Then she plunged forward once more, sucking and kissing his cock with delightful enthusiasm.

Liam gave in to the pleasure for several lovely minutes. He didn't want to come yet, however. Not this soon. He tapped her shoulder. "That's enough, sub girl. Put my cock back in my underwear and re-button my fly."

Allie looked up at him with a pout and mewed petulantly. Though Liam was both pleased and amused by her obvious reluctance to stop, he couldn't permit that sort of behavior if he was to give Allie what she claimed to crave—complete and total erotic submission.

Bending down, he slapped her right cheek, not too hard, but certainly hard enough to get her attention. With a gasp, she brought her hand to her face, her eyes widening, her lips parting, both shock and, it seemed to Liam, arousal washing over her features.

"Why did I slap you, sub Allie?"

She knit her brow, her hand still covering the spot where he'd struck her. She bit her lip, but didn't answer.

"Are you silent because you don't know? Or because you're ashamed to admit that you do know?"

Still nothing.

"Did you already forget that, as my submissive, you are to answer every direct question promptly and honestly?"

Allie dropped her hand and lowered her head a moment. Then she looked up at him with those lovely blue eyes. "I'm sorry, Sir. You took me by surprise. Face slapping is kind of a trigger for me. I have a hard time with it."

Liam nodded, filing this information away. "I understand. Now answer the question. Why did I slap you?"

"Because I was a brat, Sir." A ghost of a smile hovered over her lips. "I wasn't ready to stop when you told me to stop. I put my needs, or rather, my desires, over your direct command."

Satisfied, Liam smiled. "That's correct. Don't let it happen again." He extended his hand. When she took it, he helped pull her to her feet. "To reinforce the lesson, I'm going to take you down to my dungeon. Leave the coat but put the heels back on. I think a little discipline is in order to really bring the lesson home."

"Oooh," Allie said softly, a sound he recognized from their FaceTime conversations as one of eager anticipation with a delicious overlay of fear. He couldn't wait to turn that hot ass of hers dark red.

As he turned toward the hallway that led to the basement stairs, he froze with sudden, painful indecision. He glanced at his cane, which lay several feet away on the floor, an ugly reminder of the weakness he'd somehow managed to forget for the first time since the accident. Did he leave the cane where it lay? He could walk without it, but that made his limp so much more pronounced as he hauled his leg forward in an ungainly, graceless way.

Biting his lip so hard he nearly drew blood, he half-hopped, half-loped toward the cane. He bent quickly, grabbing it by the wrist strap and pulling it upright. He placed his right hand on the grip and turned toward Allie, avoiding her eyes in case there might be pity, or worse, there.

"Let's go," he said more harshly than he'd meant to. He turned and moved down the hallway toward the basement stairs, certain he could feel the burn of her eyes on his back, on his cane, on his limp, as she silently followed.

At the head of the stairs, he gestured for Allie to go in front of him so she wouldn't watch him descend. When she was almost at the bottom, he tucked his cane under his arm and, gripping the banisters, hopped quickly down the stairs on his right leg, using his arms to propel him forward.

Allie was staring around the space with open-mouthed wonder. "Oooh, it's *fabulous*," she breathed, the awe evident in her voice. "I can't believe you have all this amazing gear. You could open a club down here."

Liam came up beside her, looking around the room through her eyes. He hadn't been down here in months, the memories of his time with Lila too painful. At that moment, however, he could barely recall his ex-lover's face.

He looked around the room with immense satisfaction. He was quite proud of his collection of BDSM furniture, including the high-gloss wooden St. Andrew's cross with its inlay of steel along the inside of the X and the adjustable leather straps to fasten and immobilize the wrists, ankles and waist. He also had a leather-padded bondage horse, a wooden, adjustable pussy punishment beam suspended on either end from sturdy rope, an iron sleeping cage and a woven leather sling complete with stirrups in its own four-point aluminum stand.

"If you decide to stay with me, sub Allie, you'll be spending quite a lot of time down here, I promise. It's one thing to fantasize about complete erotic submission, and another to actually live it. Are you prepared to submit to whatever discipline, bondage and sadistic torture it pleases me to inflict upon you? Are you ready to suffer for me, not as a game on FaceTime, but for real?"

Allie moved closer to him, pressing her shoulder against his arm as if he could protect her from the precise thing he was offering. Instinctively, he put his arm around her and she leaned closer into his side. "Yes, Sir Liam. Yes, please, Sir. I need that. I want that. I've been waiting all my life for this."

Keeping Allie to his left so she wouldn't focus on the cane in his right hand, Liam walked her to the back of the dungeon, pride and excitement filling him as they stopped in front of a two-foot high, eight-foot long Plexiglas water submersion tub. He'd had this section of the basement covered in bathroom tile to protect the rest of the dungeon during water play. A long shower hose topped with an adjustable spray nozzle was neatly coiled on a large hook set into the wall.

Liam had never had a chance to use the tub and, until this moment, hadn't thought he ever would. He glanced at Allie, who was staring at the setup with open-mouthed, wide-eyed awe. "Do you know what this is, sub Allie?"

"I think so, Sir. It's for water bondage?" Her voice trembled slightly.

A rush of sadistic lust spurted like a drug into Liam's bloodstream, his pulse quickening, his balls tightening. "Yes. It's a submersion tub. There are so many things I could do to you. Bondage is just a part of it." He could sense Allie's coiled tension and excitement. His arm still around her, he pulled her closer.

"Imagine lying naked in the warm water, your wrists tied, your eyes blindfolded, your ears plugged, your legs spread wide. Your entire focus would be on the water; on what I'm going to do to you. I might spray your cunt with the hose until you were begging for me to let you come. To earn the privilege, you might be required to fully submerge, staying under until your Master decided to let you come up for air. You would be completely under my control, your very life in my hands."

Pulling away to gauge Allie's reaction to his words, he saw her pupils were dilated, her lips parted, her breath rapid with excitement. When she turned to face him, he saw the raw fear in her eyes, but also the desire.

"Does that excite you, sub girl?" Liam asked softly, though he knew the answer. "Does it make you wet?"

"Oh my fucking god, *yes*, Sir," Allie whispered. Her gaze shifted back to the tub, a small, sensual shudder moving through her frame.

Liam moved to stand behind her, so close they were nearly touching. Reaching around her body with his free hand, he cupped her mons and slipped one finger inside her heat, his cock pulsing hard in his jeans. She was soaking wet, her vaginal muscles gripping his finger with hot promise. Again he resisted the urge to throw her, then and there, onto the ground and thrust himself into her, rutting until he exploded.

Wantonly, she pressed her sex against his hand, a sweet, soft moan escaping her lips. Liam chuckled and made himself pull away. "Not yet, slut girl," he teased.

Placing a hand on her shoulder, he turned Allie from the tub toward the recovery couch set on the adjacent wall. "We have business to attend to first, young lady. A punishment is in order for your indiscretion upstairs."

Liam gripped the cane and swung his leg forward. It took everything he had to keep thoughts of his disability from throwing him out of the moment. He moved more quickly, outpacing Allie, desperate to get to the couch, striving to keep his expression neutral. *Stay focused,* he admonished desperately. *Put her needs above yours. Project the strength a submissive deserves from her Dom. Don't give in to your own weakness and fear.*

How easy to say; how hard to do.

Quickly he sank down in the center of the couch and set the cane behind his feet, pushing it under the couch with his heel. Once again in control, he focused on the lovely, trusting, naked girl who stood facing him in her sexy high heels.

"Get over here, sub girl. Take what's coming to you."

~*~

Allie stood rooted to the spot a few feet away from Liam, suddenly hyper-aware of herself, of her naked body, of her too-high heels, of the fact she was actually in the dungeon of the man she'd thought about virtually nonstop since they'd found each other on BDSMConnections a few weeks before.

For a strange moment, she felt as if this were a dream, just another in a series of endless fantasies as she lay alone in her bed at night, her fingers moving between her legs. But, no. This was real. She was here. And Sir Liam was watching her like a lion stalking his prey.

"Sub Allie, why are you just standing there? That's another infraction."

Sir Liam's words snapped Allie out of her reverie. She focused on his face, startled to see the sudden flash of—what was it—fear? Pain? In a moment it was gone, replaced by raised eyebrows and a downturned mouth as he drummed his fingers impatiently on the couch cushion beside him.

"I'm sorry, Sir." Allie moved quickly toward him, her heels clicking on the tiled floor. She draped herself somewhat awkwardly over his lap. He repositioned her as easily as if he were handling a rag doll, settling her so her cheek rested on the cushions to his left, her legs extended to his right.

She could feel the hard press of his cock beneath her and, unable to resist, she ground her pelvis against it, aching to feel its girth inside her.

"Stay still, sub girl." Sir Liam's tone was firm, but his cock twitched in involuntary response. "I want you to relax," he continued, his tone gentler now. His hands began to move over her shoulders and back, his fingers gently easing muscles she hadn't realized she'd been tensing. As he stroked her, Allie did relax, though her pussy still throbbed with unfulfilled need, and the excess of adrenaline from the huge risk she'd taken in appearing as she had, uninvited, still lingered in her bloodstream.

He placed a firm hand on her lower back. "I'm going to start slowly, to assess your tolerance. I am well aware that a spanking is not a punishment for a girl like you. My goal right now isn't to punish, per se, but to help you remember that when I give you a specific command, you are to obey it instantly, without hesitation and without attitude. While I'm spanking you, I'm going to ask you to do certain things. You will show me that you are obedient and willing by obeying, to the letter, whatever I ask. Do you understand?"

"Yes, Sir Liam." Allie's stomach swooped with nervous excitement. She did love a good spanking, especially draped over a sexy man's lap.

He started slowly, expertly patting, smacking and stroking her ass, the escalation of erotic pain subtle and easily tolerated. The first hard smack snapped her out of her erotic lethargy. She jerked and yelped at the sudden, sharp sting.

"Stay completely still and silent until I tell you otherwise," Sir Liam commanded, pressing his other hand firmly against her lower back. His touch soothed her, and she stilled. When the next hard smack came, she remained motionless, using breath control to process the pain without flinching.

Again and again his hand crashed with the force of a paddle over her ass, alternating cheeks in no discernable pattern, each blow harder than the last. As the pain mounted, Allie struggled to remain still, her body rigid with the effort, her breath yanked from her in rapid, staccato bursts.

"Slow your breathing," she heard Sir Liam say, though his voice seemed distant, obscured by the roar of blood pounding in her ears. He continued to hit her hard. Despite herself, she began to whimper, her body now trembling with the effort to remain still. She'd had hard spankings before, but never such a steady, forceful, unyielding beating.

She had just opened her mouth to beg, to plead for him to stop, when he said, "Lift your ass. I'm not going to stop. You are going to play with yourself while I strike you. Keep your focus on your cunt. Bring yourself to the edge of orgasm. Do *not* come. Is this clear?"

"Please, I can't do this," she begged breathlessly, squirming on his lap. "It hurts too much. It's—"

"You *can* do this." He kept her in place with his strong hand. "You asked me for this"—he delivered another stinging smack—"for exactly this, don't you remember?" *Smack.*

He was right. She had told him this precise fantasy in one of their many, long conversations late at night. She'd dreamed of being held down and spanked by a strong man until she dissolved into tears, and even then, he wouldn't stop, because he would know she needed this, even as she feared it. He would take her where she needed to go, no matter how much she resisted or protested along the way.

"I thought I wanted it," she gasped, "but—"

"Don't let fear override need, sub Allie," he interrupted. "You *need* this." Sir Liam continued to spank her, hard and steady, each stroke crashing and reverberating through her body. "You can do this," he repeated, his voice suddenly gentle, his tone encouraging. "You've just been waiting for the right man to show you your own strength, to tap into the courage I know you possess."

The spanking still hurt every bit as much as it had a moment before, but somehow his words penetrated her resistance, her fear. Yes, she *could* do this, and, more than that, she *wanted* to.

"Yes, Sir, thank you, Sir," she cried, no longer trying to stop the tears that flowed down her cheeks. She pushed through the pain, rallying her submissive courage as she lifted her ass to meet Sir Liam's hard hand. She reached beneath herself and cupped her pussy. Not only her labia, but even her inner thighs were drenched with her juices. She began to stroke herself, rubbing in time to each unyielding smack.

Oh god, oh yes, the pain, the pleasure, the arousal, the sting—it was perfect, just right, so good. She rubbed harder, faster, pleasure twisting and curling around the hot, erotic sting of his insistent, merciless palm.

Maybe this time…?

"Remove your hand and lie flat."

Wait.

What?

She was close, *so* close, she was sure of it. Closer than she'd ever been.

"Remove your hand. *Now*."

Sir Liam's firm tone caused the rising wave of orgasmic pleasure to recede. Frustrated, Allie pulled her hand away and slumped against Sir Liam's lap.

Her ass was on fire, every inch of flesh throbbing. Her clit pulsed and ached with unrequited release. A whimper of sheer frustration escaped her lips. She lay limp and exhausted as Sir Liam continued to smack her bottom.

"I know you wanted to come, sub Allie," Sir Liam said above her, his hand still crashing down on her flesh. "But you haven't earned it yet. Pleasure comes from the sheer act of submission, without expectation. Right now you're fighting through the pain, but the goal is to embrace it, to accept it, to rejoice in it. That's what I want you to try to do. Don't worry if it doesn't happen right away, but try to let go. Stop fighting. Stop white-knuckling your way through this. Uncurl your fingers; let the tension flow away. Give yourself *fully* to me. Surrender your control."

Allie opened fists she'd hadn't realized she'd made. She let out a slow, long breath and drew it in again, focusing on her breathing.

"Yes, better," Sir Liam said, his stroke lighter now against her tender, aching bottom.

A deep, sensual peace began to move through her body and spirit. She was a feather, drifting lazily through the air, gently buffeted in the spring breeze. Allie sighed against the couch cushion, unable to move a muscle.

"*That's* it. That's where I want you," Sir Liam crooned softly. He began to stroke her tortured flesh with a soft, soothing touch. "Perfect," he whispered, as Allie drifted in a warm, safe place deep inside herself.

She opened her eyes when she felt herself being lifted and then set gently back down on the sofa, still on her stomach.

"Just stay where you are," Sir Liam said from somewhere over her head. "Don't move a muscle."

That command was easy to obey, as she couldn't have moved if she tried. Her eyes closed again of their own accord and she sighed in deep contentment. She heard him moving away and then returning to her, but still she didn't move, too wrapped in the warm cocoon of submissive headspace to react.

Sir Liam placed both his hands on her ass, cupping the cheeks gently. Something cool and soothing spread over her skin as he moved his hands.

"Ah," she sighed as he gently soothed away much of the sting.

"Are you all right, Allie?" her new lover asked softly. "Can you turn over?"

Allie could have easily drifted into a blissful sleep, but that wouldn't be fair. She rolled onto her back and opened her eyes, trying to focus on

Sir Liam, who stood smiling down at her.

"Hey," he said gently. "I'm not done with you yet, sub girl."

Bending toward her, he slipped his hands beneath her body and stood, lifting her in his arms. "You did very well, sub Allie. In my dungeon, if punishment is handled with grace, there is always reward."

As he carried her across the room, his gait was uneven, his left shoulder held higher than his right, a spasm of pain moving over his face as he held her in his arms. He needed his walking cane. She wanted to wriggle out of his arms, to say, "*I can see this is hurting you. Let me down. I'll walk on my own.*" But she understood instinctively that her protest would not be welcome.

She forgot his limp and everything else when he set her into the large sling. The soft leather seat hugged her body as the swing swayed, its lightly oiled scent filling her nostrils like an aphrodisiac. The air felt cool against the hot skin of her well-spanked ass. The sensual lethargy induced by the intense spanking had completely burned away in the face of her renewed lust.

Fuck me, fuck me, fuck me. Please, please, please fuck me, she silently begged.

Echoing her thoughts, Sir Liam growled, "I can't wait another second. I have to have you now. Grip the chains behind your head and don't let go," he commanded.

Allie eagerly obeyed, watching as he placed her feet, one at a time, into the swing's stirrups and strapped her ankles into place with Velcro fasteners.

Stepping back, his eyes sweeping her naked body, he pulled his shirt over his head and tossed it aside. His shoulders and chest bulged with muscle, his abs neatly arranged in a classic, hard six-pack. His chest hair was dark and curly, a tantalizing line tapering down his flat stomach to below the waist of his jeans.

He moved between her legs, forced wide by her position, and reached for his jeans, pulling the fly open with a single yank of his hand. She watched hungrily as he lowered his jeans and underwear, eager to see him naked. She was disappointed when, as he'd done upstairs, he stopped at mid-thigh, revealing only enough of himself to get the job done.

She forgot her disappointment as he moved closer, guiding his cock to her entrance. He knew already from their many conversations and emails that she was disease-free and on the pill, and she knew he, too, was clean. She was glad he trusted her, and didn't try to whip out a condom at such a moment, a real buzzkill in her book.

He leaned over her and kissed her mouth, his hard, lovely body covering hers. The head of his cock nudged against her and she arched forward as best she could in her tethered position. She groaned with pleasure as he entered her in one long, insistent push.

He closed his hands over her wrists and used the swing to pull her forward onto his long, thick shaft. "Christ," he breathed, his eyes closing. "You're perfect."

If only that were true.

CHAPTER 5

Allie opened her eyes. Weak sunlight filtered through the half-open slats of the blinds, washing the room in oyster-shell pink. Her cheek was nestled against Liam's warm chest, his arm flung loosely around her shoulders. His heartbeat was slow and steady beneath her ear, his breathing deep.

Stealthily, she slipped from beneath his arm. As she moved, he turned his head and sighed. Allie froze, waiting to see if she had awakened him, but he remained still. Quietly, she lifted herself on an elbow and regarded his face, which rested in profile on the pillow. He had a slight bump on the bridge of his nose. His eyelashes were long and dark against his pale skin, his brows thick and straight. She liked the way the stubble shadowed his strong jaw and square chin. She resisted the urge to stroke her finger along the line of his bones.

After the incredible session in the dungeon, Allie, who had been too nervous to eat much over the course of the day, had been ravenous. Liam didn't have that much in his refrigerator, but he did have a large and very satisfactory supply of ice cream, as well as some bananas. Dressed in one of Liam's soft, faded T-shirts and nothing else, Allie had sat on a barstool, watching him slice the overripe bananas and pile them high with scoops of French vanilla ice cream, hot fudge he'd heated in the microwave and a healthy squirt of whipped cream. Allie didn't usually go in for such sweet, messy concoctions, but each gooey bite had tasted more delicious than the last, and before she knew it she had finished the entire bowl.

Exhausted from the long day and amazing night, she hadn't protested when Liam suggested they go to bed. They didn't go straight to sleep however, and Allie smiled now as she recalled Liam's gentle, tender lovemaking in the dark, a perfect counterpoint to the very intense experience in the dungeon.

Now the blanket was bunched at the end of the bed, the sheet covering Liam to the waist. Allie gripped the edge of the sheet and carefully began to draw it downward, eager to see his naked body in the daylight. She was both wildly curious and half afraid of what she might see.

Allie jerked her hand away as Liam sat up abruptly, his eyes flying open. He furrowed his brows as he stared at her, as if he didn't know who she was, or how she had appeared in his bed.

"I'm sorry. I didn't mean to startle you." A wash of heat moved over her cheeks.

Liam's scowl softened at once into an apologetic smile. "Sorry. I must have been dreaming." The smile broadened into a happy grin as he held out his arms. "Come here, you."

Allie snuggled once more against him. "I hope it was a good dream. I've been having dreams of my own, very explicit ones that involve you." She giggled as she placed her palm lightly over the sheet that covered Liam's erection.

"Oh, you were, were you?" In a sudden movement, Liam gripped Allie's wrist and flipped her onto her back. Grabbing her other wrist, he stretched her arms over her head, pressing them into the mattress as he rolled over and covered her body with his.

Allie parted her lips eagerly for his kiss. She could feel his hard cock nudging at her thigh. She tried to shift beneath him, spreading her legs and angling her body to receive him. He pulled away from her with a laugh. "Oh, no you don't. You don't call the shots here, young lady. Last night was free time. Starting today, you have to earn my cock."

"But—" Allie began to protest, her cunt wet and throbbing. She tried to pull her arms free but he held tight.

"No buts," he interrupted. "Last night you said you wanted to submit to me. This morning we will discuss precisely what that submission entails." He let her go and lifted himself from her. Turning away, he swung his legs over his side of the bed. To her chagrin, Allie saw that he was wearing pajama pants, though she was pleased to see evidence of his erection still tenting the material.

Perhaps in an effort to soften his words, he added, "Last night was fabulous, and I'm so glad you're here." He flashed a heartbreakingly sweet smile at her, and Allie smiled back, her heart squeezing in her chest. "But this morning we need to discuss some ground rules. It's one thing to connect online and in video chats. Real life can be quite different. I believe you want a genuine and intense submissive experience, but we need to make sure we are on the same page as to what that means for each of us individually, and as Master and sub."

This made sense to Allie, and she nodded as she, too, climbed out of the bed. Liam grabbed his walking cane and moved toward the bathroom. Allie watched him go, noting that he barely limped when using the cane. Her mind veered back to the night before when he'd carried her in his arms, his mouth compressed in a thin line of determined concentration, the pain stark in his face.

He glanced back at her now, and Allie quickly averted her gaze, not wanting to make him self-conscious. "Come on," he said. "Let's get washed up and have some coffee. I can't think until I've had my coffee."

Allie, so nervous and excited when she'd planned her arrival at his doorstep the night before, hadn't even brought so much as a toothbrush with her from the hotel. Liam, fortunately, had a spare. As she was brushing her teeth, he came up behind her. She saw him regarding her in the mirror, his head tilted in appraisal.

He reached out and lightly drew a finger over her left butt cheek. "You have some nice bruises there, sub girl. You took quite a spanking last night."

"Oh, let me see!" A jolt of excitement shot through Allie as she pivoted and twisted her head back to regard herself in the mirror. There were several small bruises on either cheek, one rather large one on the left side. She bit her lip as she gazed at her mottled butt cheeks. A tiny part of her brain protested in outrage that she had allowed herself to be hit like this, but the overwhelming majority of her cerebral committee gave her a standing ovation.

"They're beautiful, aren't they?" Liam said, wonderment moving over his features. He shook his head slowly. "I'm so impressed with the courage of a true submissive," he added as pride suffused its way through Allie's being like pure, life-giving sunshine.

Liam met her eye in the mirror and winked at her as he gave her a light pat on the bottom.

"Okay, then," he said. "I'll have a shower and shave after breakfast. Why don't you jump in the shower while I make the coffee? We can figure out about getting your stuff from the hotel later. Meanwhile I think I'd like to keep you naked." He moved his eyes appraisingly over Allie's body, and her nipples stiffened beneath his gaze.

As Allie showered, she toyed briefly with the idea of touching herself, nearly certain she'd be able to come with her own fingers, as aroused as she was. But she decided against it, not wanting to keep Liam waiting.

When she walked into the kitchen, she was surprised but pleased to find a plate of scrambled eggs and buttered toast waiting on the table for her, along with a large mug of dark strong coffee, to which she promptly added plenty of cream and sugar. It was a little odd to sit naked at breakfast, but at the same time it was exciting. She was there not only as Liam's new lover, but as his submissive, with all that entailed.

Lifting a forkful of buttery eggs to her mouth, Allie chewed and swallowed, her stomach grateful for the protein after last night's sugar and fat fest. "I don't usually even eat breakfast, but this is really good."

"Glad you approve," Liam said with a laugh.

It had begun to rain, the sky slate gray outside the kitchen window. Liam, following her gaze, said, "Welcome to Oregon," with an apologetic shrug that segued into an evil smile. "Not that I'm planning to let you out of the house anytime soon. Speaking of which, how long are you going to be able to stay? A day, a week, a year?"

Allie grinned. "My return ticket is open-ended. I've definitely cleared the schedule for a week's absence back home. I fulfilled all the outstanding commitments I had to get done before I left. I have a part-time assistant who will be able to handle any online orders for me until I get back. She's got the bulk of the inventory, and she'll let me know if there are any problems or anything."

"Excellent," Liam said. "A week is a good length of time for you to determine if the kind of D/s experience I can offer you is what you really want. I do ask that you wait until the end of that period to decide. What I mean is, some of this is going to be hard for you, or at the very least new for you, and I want you to give it a chance. We have the added advantage of already having forged a genuine connection in the weeks we've known each other, but actually being together, actually living this lifestyle 24/7, will take some adjustment."

"24/7?" Allie said, her voice coming out as a squeak as her stomach executed a loop-de-loop of nervous excitement.

Liam shook his head. "I don't mean 24/7 slave Master stuff. We've already agreed that's not the lifestyle either of us is seeking. I mean, though our exchange of power will be primarily erotic, there will always be the underlying dynamic of Dom and sub between us. While I don't expect you to be at my beck and call every second of the day, I do expect you to submit to me when it pleases me and how it pleases me. If I give you certain parameters under which I expect you to function, you will observe those parameters at all times, even if we're not together at a particular moment."

"Like what do you mean?" Allie asked, confused.

"For example"—a hint of smile curved Liam's sensual mouth—"for the duration of this week, you will not touch yourself sexually without my express permission or command. In other words, for as long as you belong to me, you are never to masturbate when you are alone, unless I have expressly directed you to do so."

"Oh," Allie said softly, her clit instantly hard, a sudden, perverse desire to touch herself making her fingers tingle. To distract herself, she lifted her coffee mug to her lips and took a sip.

"We'll talk more after breakfast," Liam said. "I'm having a second cup. Would you like one?"

"No, I'm good, thanks," Allie replied. Too excited and agitated to eat any more, she continued to sip at her coffee while Liam plowed through a large mound of eggs and half a dozen pieces of bacon.

Finally he set his fork on his empty plate and pushed back from the table. "Hey, you barely ate. I'm sorry, I should have asked if you wanted something different." He scratched his head as if thinking and offered, "I think there's one more banana. Would you rather have that?"

"No, no. I'm fine, really," Allie said quickly. "I don't usually eat that much breakfast."

"Okay, if you're sure."

Allie nodded that she was.

Reaching for his cane, Liam pushed himself upright. "If you don't mind," he said, "could you load the dishwasher and put things away while I take a quick shower? Then we'll talk about our expectations and intentions going forward."

Allie, looked down at herself and then back up at Liam with a grin. "Uh, you got an apron or something? I don't want to mess up my outfit."

Liam grinned back. "It's on a hook on the inside of the pantry door." He nodded in that direction. "When you're done, you can wait for me in the living room. There are floor cushions under the large sofa. Pull one out and kneel up at attention."

"Yes, Sir," Allie replied softly.

As she washed up, she thought about what her expectations and intentions actually were. Truth to tell, beyond rather vague fantasies of intense dungeon scenes, she hadn't gotten much past arriving on his doorstep and offering herself to him. She had been so caught up in the passion and excitement of the night before she hadn't considered what would happen next.

Allie was just rehanging the apron on its hook when she heard guitar chords, accompanied by the unmistakable sound of a cell phone vibrating against wood. Grabbing a dishtowel, she approached the table, not sure what to do.

Liam appeared at that moment, shirtless in a pair of faded jeans, rubbing the back of his head with a towel. "There you are," he said, apparently addressing his phone. He grabbed it and, after a brief glance at the screen, took the call.

"How am I? Let's see, is this question for before or after I kill you?"

Liam laughed. "It's Matt," he mouthed silently in Allie's direction, as the person on the other end spoke into his ear. "Yeah, sure, okay, yes, you can stop by, but don't overstay your welcome, if you know what I mean." He winked at Allie, still grinning.

He listened a while longer and then, placing his hand over the phone, he said to Allie, "Matt and Bonnie want to swing by, just to say hi. They want to know if they should stop by the hotel and pick up your things. Apparently the room was made in Matt's name, so it shouldn't be a problem." He lifted his eyebrows in question.

"Yes, that would be good," Allie replied, suddenly pleased at the thought of meeting Bonnie Wilson, the woman who had put this whole amazing trip together.

When he'd hung up, she asked, "Uh, what about what I'm wearing, or rather *not* wearing? Should I go get my raincoat?"

"Maybe I'll present you just as you are," Liam said with a sly grin, his eyes moving hungrily over her naked form. Allie started to open her mouth in protest, but before she could speak, Liam added, "I think not. Not yet. I'm not ready to share you in that way, not even with Matt and Bonnie."

Allie closed her mouth, relieved. While she didn't object in principle to appearing naked in front of others, and indeed had done it many times at the BDSM clubs, she wasn't quite ready to do so in front of Liam's friends, sight unseen.

Liam put his hands on her shoulders and leaned down to kiss her on the forehead. "Come into my bedroom. I'll find something you can wear while they're here. After they leave, we can pick up where we left off."

"Is that a promise or a threat?" Allie quipped.

"Which do you want it to be?" Liam asked softly, his hand moving from her shoulder to her throat.

Allie forgot how to speak as his fingers tightened beneath her jaw. He dipped his head once more, this time kissing her hard on the mouth. When he finally let go, she managed breathlessly, "Both, please, Sir."

~*~

Liam glanced at Allie when the doorbell rang. He smiled at her. She smiled back, though he could see she was a little nervous. She was dressed in one of his old college T-shirts and a pair of his gym shorts. Even in the over-large clothing, she looked sexy as hell, her pert nipples pressing against the much-washed cotton of the shirt, her long, pretty legs tucked beneath her on the couch.

"Come in," he called toward the door. "It's open."

The door opened and shut. A moment later, Matt and Bonnie appeared from the foyer, both smiling widely. Bonnie held a bottle of champagne. Matt pulled a wheeled suitcase behind him, two plastic grocery bags over his arm. Liam stood, moving toward Matt. As they embraced, Matt murmured, "Hey, buddy. I hope it's all good."

"Better than good," Liam affirmed. "Thank you for doing this."

Allie stood as Bonnie approached her with a smile. "Allie, I'm so glad to meet you. I'm so glad you came!" Bonnie opened her arms and the two of them embraced as if they were long-lost sisters.

"Me, too," Allie said, once they'd let each other go. "Liam is lucky to have such good friends."

"And we're lucky to have him," Bonnie replied, turning to include Liam in the radiant warmth of her smile. "I hope you're treating this lovely sub properly, Liam."

"You'll have to ask her," Liam retorted with a grin, though his gut clenched in a moment of apprehension. He wouldn't be able to hide his scars from Allie forever—at least not the physical ones, and then what?

"Very properly," Allie affirmed, moving to stand beside Liam, who slid his arm around her shoulders and pulled her close.

Liam nodded toward the bottle in Bonnie's hand. "Isn't it a little early to start drinking?"

"Champagne to celebrate new beginnings," Bonnie said. "We can always add orange juice if you like."

"Hey, it's five o'clock somewhere, right?" Matt interjected with a laugh. "I'll get the glasses. I'll put this stuff away, too. Bonnie bought you guys enough provisions so you won't have to leave the house for a week, if you don't want to." Without waiting for a response, he headed off to the kitchen.

Bonnie handed Liam the champagne bottle. "He's exaggerating. It's just a few basics. I know how you stock, or rather, don't stock your fridge, and you have a guest now, so…"

She trailed off, looking suddenly uncertain, which made Liam want to leap instantly to her defense. "That was really thoughtful of you, Bonnie," he said sincerely. "Thank you, truly." He glanced at Allie and turned back to Bonnie. "More than that, thank you for this chance—for doing what I couldn't."

Bonnie smiled and said softly, "You could have. I just speeded things up a bit." In a louder voice, she added, "Don't worry, we're only going to stay long enough for a quick toast." She glanced at Allie, still smiling. "Allie and I can catch up later, when she gives me a complete critique regarding your capabilities as a Dom."

"Oh, no she won't," Liam retorted. "That's what gags are for."

"Like that would stop me," Allie joked. "I'd just use sign language."

When Matt returned with the glasses, Liam popped the cork on the champagne and poured everyone a small amount. Matt and Bonnie settled on the couch, Allie next to Liam on the adjacent loveseat, their thighs touching. Matt lifted his glass in a toast, and the other three did likewise. "To old friends and new discoveries," he said. They clinked glasses.

As they sipped, they made small talk about Allie's flight, her jewelry business, Matt and Bonnie's experience in the BDSM scene and Liam's work as a grant writer. He had been so focused on their D/s connection he hadn't really paid sufficient attention to Allie's professional life. Listening now as Bonnie and Matt drew her out, Liam was impressed not only with Allie's artistic talent, but with her obvious business acumen and quick mind. Allie spoke easily with his friends, who both seemed to accept her immediately and completely. While deeply grateful that the three people he valued most in this world were getting along so well, Liam was eager to have Allie once more fully to himself.

True to their word, after only about twenty minutes, Bonnie touched Matt's arm and they communicated telepathically in the way people who had been together a long time sometimes did. They rose of one accord and Matt said, "We have to be going." He grinned, adding, "I'd tell you two to behave, but that wouldn't be any fun, would it?"

"None at all," Liam agreed with a grin as he lightly squeezed Allie's smooth, bare thigh.

Allie and he walked the couple to the door. Bonnie gave Allie another sisterly hug and whispered something in Allie's ear that made her smile.

Matt leaned close to Liam and said softly, "I know we pulled a fast one with all our behind-the-scenes interfering, but you know it's because we love you, right?"

"I do know," Liam said soberly. "And thank you for doing it. Thanks for taking that risk for me."

"You're more than welcome," Matt replied. "You've taken the first step. Now just keep moving forward, okay? Give her, and more importantly, yourself, a chance."

~*~

When the front door closed behind Matt and Bonnie, Liam put his arm around Allie and led her back into the living room. "It's time, sub girl. Take off those clothes and kneel as I instructed you earlier, hands behind your head." Something in Liam's countenance and demeanor had changed, a subtle but real shift into a dominant mode to which the submissive in Allie instantly responded.

"Yes, Sir Liam." Allie crouched beside the large sofa and ran her hand beneath it. She found and pulled out a large, flat cushion covered in pale blue silk. She positioned herself on the cushion and lifted her arms, lacing her fingers behind her neck. She drew in a deep breath and let it out slowly, embracing the sense of peace that settled over her in this submissive pose.

Sir Liam sat on the sofa directly in front of her. Leaning forward, he stroked her cheek lightly with two fingers. "From this moment forward, you belong to me. We've talked a lot online and on the phone about what you're seeking in a D/s relationship, but I want to make sure we both fully understand the parameters of the next few days as we explore this together. I know what you want, or at least I know what you've said you want. You are seeking an intense, hardcore masochistic experience and complete submission within the context of an erotic exchange of power. Do I have that right?"

"You do, Sir," Allie whispered, his words buzzing like electric currents over her skin and sending eddies of nervous excitement through her gut.

Sir Liam nodded. "Good. I want that, too. I want to take you to the edge. I want to explore your boundaries, and then take you past them, just a little. In order to do this, it is absolutely essential that we have open communication every step of the way. While I will call the shots and handle your submissive training as I see fit, I need to fully understand your reactions, your needs, your desires. I need your input, and most importantly, I need your honesty. There should be no secrets between us within the context of our D/s exploration."

Secrets.

But there are always secrets, aren't there?

Was a lie of omission still a lie?

"Allie?" Sir Liam was regarding her quizzically, his penetrating gaze suddenly unnerving.

She looked down, saying nothing.

"What is it, sub Allie?" Sir Liam persisted. He placed his index finger beneath her chin, forcing her to look up. "What's going on in your head? Do you have a problem with something I said? If so, let's talk it through."

Allie shook her head. "No. No, it's—nothing, Sir."

He regarded her a moment longer, as if willing her to say more. Though, thankfully, he didn't press. Finally, he glanced at his watch, which had an old-fashioned oval-shaped face on a worn black leather band. "You may lower your arms now. Put your hands behind your back."

Glad for the distraction, Allie let her arms fall and reached behind her back to clasp her hands together, aware of how this forced her breasts to jut forward. Sir Liam moved his gaze slowly over her body. Her nipples tingled beneath his scrutiny, her cunt gently throbbing.

"Okay, then," he said. "It's early days, yet. But I want you to promise me you'll feel free to speak at any time if something doesn't feel right, or if you're afraid, or you need something you aren't getting, or you can't handle something I'm asking of you. That isn't to say I'll necessarily stop what I'm doing, but I need to hear what you are experiencing. I need to take your feelings, your desires and your fears into consideration as I develop your submissive regimen over the next few days. Being a sub does not mean being a passive recipient of whatever I decide to mete out. I want a dynamic relationship with a thinking, actively involved submissive, is that clear? Are we on the same page, Allie? Will you promise to remain open with me?"

"Yes," Allie affirmed, tucking that one niggling secret back into its hidey hole. "I promise."

Sir Liam stood. "Good. The first thing I want to do this morning is to assess both your sexual reactions to stimulus and explore further your tolerance for erotic pain. I think some nice cunt torture should fit both bills, hmm?"

"Oooh," Allie breathed. "*Yes*, Sir."

At the basement stairs, Sir Liam again indicated Allie should go first. She turned at the bottom to watch him as he swung down the stairs with a dancer's grace, the walking cane tucked somehow beneath one of his arms, his muscles bulging as he used the bannisters for support. She almost said something aloud about how impressive he looked, but sensed he might not appreciate it.

He led her to a high leather spanking bench set on steel legs, knee rests running along both sides. "I want you to lie on your back on the bondage horse," Sir Liam said. "I'm going to tie you down with your legs spread wide so you won't be tempted to accidentally move while I'm torturing you. Place your feet flat on the leg rests and then lift your hips so I can slide a wedge under your ass. I want full access to that beautiful cunt of yours."

Her heart beating fast, Allie climbed onto the horse and settled herself on it as instructed. Sir Liam moved out of her line of sight, returning a moment later with a padded wedge, which he pushed beneath her raised bottom.

Allie sighed with pleasure as Sir Liam tethered her wrists over her head against the front end of the horse. How she adored being bound—it was at once exhilarating and soothing. Her breath quickened as he placed leather straps over her body—one just beneath her breasts, one across her hips and one over each thigh to keep her from closing her legs. He worked quietly and efficiently, his touch gentle but sure as he secured the straps with clips he attached to the O-rings along the perimeter of the bench.

"Can you move?" he queried, his eyes glittering with undisguised lust and power. He was shirtless, but still in his jeans, his feet bare.

Allie tried to close her legs. She pulled against the straps that held her arms over her head. She attempted to twist free of bonds that held her down. She couldn't move an inch. "No, Sir," she said, her heart pounding in her ears. Though she trusted Sir Liam intrinsically, she couldn't stop the shiver of genuine fear that coursed through her body at the realization she was completely at his mercy, naked, bound and offered up to him for whatever he chose to do to her.

There was a free-standing rack beside the bench that held dozens of canes of varying lengths and thicknesses, along with single tail whips, floggers and paddles. Sir Liam selected a small, thick cane about half an inch in diameter. On closer inspection, Allie saw it was actually a bundle of thin wooden skewers, banded together at either end with red string.

"Simple, but quite effective," Sir Liam said, his smile cruel. He drew the sharp points of the bound skewers along her thigh and stomach. "Are you afraid, sub Allie?" he murmured in a low, sensual voice.

Allie sucked in a sudden, sharp breath, her heart jolting with fear. "Yes," she hissed. "I'm afraid of canes. I know I didn't put that on the hard limits, but I've—I've never let anyone use one on me before, Sir. They seem so brutal." An image of the flayed, bloody back of a man in Singapore she'd once seen in an article about corporal punishment planted itself firmly in her mind's eye.

"Improperly handled, they can be," Sir Liam agreed. "Luckily for you, I know what I'm doing." Apparently taking pity on her, he added in a gentler tone, "It's okay, sub Allie. This is different than an actual caning on your ass. Cunt canings require more delicate torture, and I'm fully aware of that, trust me."

"Yes, Sir Liam," Allie whispered. She did trust him, and in spite of her fear, perhaps partially because of it, she wanted to experience what he was offering. Nevertheless, an involuntary shudder moved through her body at the thought of a cunt caning. "But I'm still afraid, Sir."

Sir Liam nodded soberly, his green eyes staring into her soul. "Good. Fear makes you focus, and I want you to pay attention. I'm going to start lightly, and ratchet up the intensity of the beating based on what I think you can tolerate. I want you to suffer for me but you needn't stay silent. You are free to speak. You are free to cry out. In fact, I want you to tell me if you think it's too much, or if you're having a hard time. I will listen, and then I will decide whether to continue. We're still new, however, and it's possible I'll misjudge. If you absolutely need it, use your safeword. But remember, that is a last resort. You say *diamond*, and all action ceases. Remain strong, summon all your submissive courage, and together we will push the boundaries of your masochistic longing."

He moved to stand by Allie's head. He touched the flat of the small cane to her lips. "Kiss it," he ordered. "Kiss the cane I'm going to beat your cunt with."

Allie pursed her lips into a kiss against the bamboo and tried to fill her lungs, which seemed as if they'd collapsed.

"Breathe," Sir Liam said, watching her face. "Harness your fear, sub girl. Remember, don't fight the pain. Embrace it."

"Yes," Allie whispered, his words calming her, reminding her this was where she wanted to be; where she'd dreamed of being since the moment she'd met him online. She released a long breath of surrender as Liam moved around the bench to stand beside her raised pelvis.

The cane landed lightly at first, as promised, a stinging kiss against her already swollen, moist labia. Then came a much sharper blow, the sting shooting through her like fire, igniting something hot and urgent deep in her core. "Ah!" Allie cried, jerking against her bonds. He struck her again, just as hard, and Allie's cry segued into a scream. Sweat broke out along her upper lip and beneath her arms. She was panting, her cunt throbbing.

"Shall I continue, sub Allie?"

Allie blew out a breath. *No, no, no, no,* a part of her cried. *Yes, yes, yes, yes,* shouted another. *Don't fuck it up, Allie. You can do this!*

"Yes, please, Sir," she finally managed, her voice trembling but resolute.

With a satisfied nod, he resumed the caning, each stroke a little harder than the last until she was whimpering steadily, desperate to close her legs. "Oh god, oh god, oh god," she chanted. "I can't..."

"Do you need me to stop, sub Allie?" He struck harder, a searing blow that caught her clit and made her see stars.

"Yes!" she screamed, tears streaming down her cheeks. "Ow, ow, ow, it hurts! Oh god, I can't do it. I'm afraid."

"Push past the fear, sub girl." Sir Liam urged, "Don't think about what you *want* right now, but what you *need*. Do you need this, Allie? Do you need what I'm giving you now?"

Oh, my god. That's it.

All at once Allie understood something she hadn't been able to articulate, even to herself. Until now, while the interaction with Sir Liam had been wonderful and intense, it had been, at least to some degree, a fantasy. She was the online sub princess, discovered by an internet Dom Charming there to sweep her off her feet.

But this went beyond that. Sir Liam wasn't enacting a scene. He was claiming her with this caning—it was that simple. He was moving past the purely sexual allure masochism had always held for her to something deeper—something more sublime.

"Yes," she cried, her voice hoarse. "Yes, please, Sir. I need it."

As she said the words, something inside her, some last vestige of resistance, broke away, like a dam crumbling beneath the force of floodwaters. The pain, while still hot and immediate, submerged into dark, sweet pleasure. Allie moaned and sighed, melting against the padded leather in a pool of aching desire. Sir Liam continued to cane her tender, throbbing cunt, but it was gentler now, steadily easing until it was just a whisper of bamboo stroking the tender folds.

She opened her eyes when something touched her lips. It was the cane. She kissed it and it was withdrawn. Her eyes fluttered shut and she drifted, her spirit somewhere outside her body, a deep, pervasive peace settling over her like a warm blanket.

"Beautiful," she heard Sir Liam say from somewhere far away.

She opened her eyes again as Sir Liam gathered her into his arms. She hadn't been aware when he'd released the leather bonds that held her down. Her pussy still throbbed, the rest of her body limp and utterly relaxed.

Sir Liam bent over her and slid his arms beneath her. "Put your arms around my neck," he instructed. "I'm going to carry you to the recovery couch."

It took all Allie's effort to muster the strength needed to jumpstart her muscles into action as Liam lifted her into his strong arms. Again, she was aware of his uneven gait and jerking shoulders as he moved, but she was too physically spent to even think of offering to walk herself. Her bones, she was sure, had turned to jelly.

Sir Liam settled on the couch with Allie still in his arms. She came slowly to herself as he kissed her—sweet butterfly kisses on her eyelids, her cheeks, her forehead, her closed lips, her chin.

"How do you feel?" he asked, and Allie realized she'd begun to drift again in a peaceful ocean of quiet joy. She forced her eyes to open and saw he was smiling tenderly at her.

She smiled back. "I feel like heaven," she said truthfully. "Thank you, Sir Liam. Thank you for..." She paused, at a loss at how to express the myriad feelings coursing through her at that moment. Gratitude, empowerment, joy, wild attraction...love? No, too soon. Way, way, way too soon to speak of love. "For everything," she finished, lamely.

"Thank you, sub Allie, for trusting me so completely and so soon. I'm very impressed. You have incredible potential."

Allie smiled up at her new lover as she savored his praise. "Thank you, Sir."

He lifted her from his lap and set her beside him. Leaning over, Sir Liam turned to a mini refrigerator next to the couch. Opening the door, he pulled out a cold bottle of water, unscrewed the cap and handed the bottle to Allie. Allie, who hadn't known she was thirsty, drank until it was empty.

Liam took the bottle from her and set it down on top of the small refrigerator. "Now," he said. "We need to finish our discussion from upstairs. You will start by telling me what you withheld while you were on your knees. What is it, Allie? What is it you're not telling me?"

CHAPTER 6

The dreamy, sexy look on Allie's face vanished. She looked up sharply at Liam, her eyes widening, her teeth suddenly worrying her lower lip. "What?" she asked, a defensive tone in her words. "What do you mean?"

Letting the tone slide for the moment, Liam said calmly, "There's something you're not telling me. You're keeping something from me. Am I mistaken?" He looked into her eyes, certain he was correct, though he didn't want to bully the answer from her. If this was going to work between them, the gift of her submission had to be voluntary. He would not wrest it from her.

Allie was silent for several long moments as she regarded him. Finally, she swallowed hard, a resolute look coming over her features. "Okay," she said, "you're right. I admit it. I have a secret."

Liam waited, sudden thoughts of another man or a terminal disease flashing through his mind. He pushed these thoughts away, refusing to jump to conclusions. "Go on. You can tell me. You're safe here."

Tears filled her eyes, and she blinked them rapidly away. She tossed back her tousled hair from her face with a flip of her head and then blew out a long breath. "I'm broken," she finally said.

Liam didn't respond at once, not sure what she meant. She appeared quite intact to him, no crushed bones, no scars. She was perfection itself, as far as he could see. "I'm sorry, what?" Perhaps he had misheard.

Allie gave a small, self-conscious laugh. "Well, not literally. I have this little problem. I can't... I don't..." She trailed off.

"Go on," Liam urged gently. "You can't..."

She blew out another breath and then said in a sudden rush of words, "I can't orgasm with a man. There. I said it." She met his gaze head-on, something like defiance entering her expression.

Liam blinked in confusion. "What do you mean? What about last night? You were amazing. It was incredible..." He trailed off, trying to reconcile her words with his experience. It had been ideal, both of them hurtling toward climax at the same moment, the grip of her cunt muscles, her ragged breathing, her sweet, breathy sighs...

Liam looked back slowly, understanding finally dawning. "Oh, I see."

Allie's face crumpled, her hands clenching into fists in her lap. "So, now you know. I'm not only broken, I'm a liar. I've been doing it forever. I know just how to fake it. I know the sounds to make, and the way to breathe so that I actually increase my heart rate." She barked a small, mirthless laugh. "Sometimes I'm so good I actually fool myself. Last night"—she looked up at him, her expression beseeching—"I was so close. I was right there, teetering on the edge and I really thought *this* was it, that it would finally happen for me."

She dropped her gaze again, and Liam saw a teardrop splash onto her leg. "But it's no use. There's something wrong with me. I can't connect. I keep hoping that something, like that incredible spanking just before the sex would, you know, be enough to get me there, but it never is. It never has been."

Liam's heart squeezed with compassion. He placed his hands over her closed fists. "Allie, you're not broken. It's okay."

Allie's hands remained balled tight beneath his. "You don't get it. I lied. A D/s relationship is supposed to be based on honesty, and I've started us out with lies. I lied by omission this whole time we've been talking and interacting all these weeks. I compounded the lies last night. I lied with my body and my actions—with what I allowed you to believe, with what I wanted you to believe." She looked up at him, another tear rolling down her cheek. "I totally get it if you need me to leave now."

For a second Liam didn't know what she meant. Leave where? The basement dungeon? What was she talking about? Then he understood. He shook his head and turned her hands over, slipping his fingers between hers and forcing them to unfurl.

"Allie, why in the world would I want you to leave?" When Allie didn't respond, he said, "Let me ask you a question. Have you told anyone else this secret of yours?"

Allie shook her head, looking miserable. Liam reached for a strand of hair that had fallen into her face and tucked it behind her ear. "It's not exactly something I'm proud of. Not only that I'm broken, but that I'm a big fat liar."

In spite of himself, and in spite of Allie's very real distress, Liam couldn't help but smile. "Allie, sweetheart, big and fat are not words I would ever associate with you." She looked up with a wan expression and he let his smile slide away. "I'm sorry, I don't mean to make light of this at all. I can see it's something that's been weighing heavily on you. And I'm sorry that you felt the need to pretend for me. But I'm also very glad that you told me the truth. I appreciate what an act of courage it was just now to confide in me. And it's also a beautiful act of submission, Allie. I'm grateful that you feel safe with me, safe enough to confide your secret."

"So what now? How can I be your sex slave if I can't even orgasm?"

Allie forced a laugh, but Liam sensed the seriousness behind her question.

Liam shrugged philosophically. "You know what they say, it's not just the destination, it's the journey. I think that's especially true of BDSM."

When Allie looked puzzled, he continued, "What I mean is, not everyone, men included, are necessarily able to achieve orgasm with a partner or even by themselves. That doesn't mean they can't have an amazing experience along the way."

"Oh, I get it," Allie said, a genuine smile lifting her lips. "You know, you're right. I'd take a good flogging over an orgasm any day of the week."

Liam nodded, though he silently promised himself to change this dynamic for his sub girl. If he had his way, she would no longer have to choose. Aloud, he said, "Let me ask you this, can you orgasm with your own hand? By yourself, when you're masturbating?"

Allie shrugged. "I guess so. I mean, I think so. Something happens, but it's definitely not the earth-moving, mind-shattering experience you hear about. It's more like scratching an itch, if you know what I mean. I figure there has to be more, but I've certainly never found it." She frowned, adding, "Like I said, I'm broken. I don't work properly. My lady parts are defective." She laughed as she said these last words and they sounded so silly that Liam laughed too.

"Your lady parts are just fine, let me assure you," he said, still smiling. "Listen to me," he added earnestly. "You're not broken. I'm sure of it. You just need more. You need the intensity of experience that a D/s relationship can provide, but more than that, you need to learn to trust."

Allie knitted her brows, a small worry line appearing between them. "So that's it? You think you can fix me?"

Liam laughed again as he shook his head. "Silly girl, you're not broken, so there's nothing to fix. As to your having an orgasm or not, I don't think it's something we need to be especially focused on at this stage."

"What do you mean?" Allie sounded incredulous. "I'd call this a pretty crucial issue, a core problem. We're about to spend a week together delving into an intense D/s relationship. Correct me if I'm wrong, but isn't my ability to orgasm fairly key in this equation?"

Liam nodded slowly as he thought how to phrase his words. "Sexual performance and sexual obedience are important in a D/s relationship, certainly. But they are only part of the equation, as you call it." He reached for her hand and brought it to his lips so he could kiss the fleshy pad of her palm.

After a moment he looked up at her. "I'm not sure where, but somewhere along the line you apparently got the impression that you have to be perfect." He waved his hand toward his left leg and grimaced. "Obviously, *I'm* far from perfect." Distressed by her sudden sympathetic expression, he hurried on. "What I'm trying to say is, I don't expect or require perfection. What I do expect is your submission, your best effort and your honesty."

He took both her hands in his. "As we move forward, our focus will not be on making you orgasm. In fact, I'm tempted to forbid you to orgasm." He grinned, thinking it over as he added, "That's actually not a bad idea. I might take you to the edge of arousal and then forbid you to come." Dropping her hands, he rubbed his together, some deliciously evil ideas rapidly forming in his brain.

"You *don't* want me to orgasm?" Allie asked, wrinkling her nose in apparent confusion.

Liam regarded her. "Perhaps, eventually, I may permit it. But I'm thinking for now, our focus will not be on whether or not you climax. Our focus will continue to be what we outlined before—stretching your boundaries while exposing you to a heightened level of erotic and masochistic experience. If, in the process, you feel a need to orgasm, you will ask me permission. I may or may not grant that permission. It will be entirely up to me."

Warming to his topic, Liam continued, "As of this moment, you give full control of your orgasms to your Master. You no longer need to pretend, to lie, to try, or to fail. In fact, you may not do any of those things. What you will do is open yourself submissively to me. Remember, as your Master, I'm also your safe place. That means if you get scared or feel like you need to revert back to that less honest, less open place you're used to inhabiting, you reject that. You come to me first and talk with me about it. Okay, Allie? Do you think you can do that? Do you want to do that?"

Allie stared at him, her lips softly parted, her chest rising and falling, no hint of the sassy sub girl in evidence. Her eyes were bright with grateful tears that touched Liam's heart. She slipped from the couch and lowered herself to her knees in front of him. "Yes, Sir. Yes, Sir Liam, I want to do that. More than anything I've ever wanted in my life." She wrapped her arms around his legs and rested her cheek on his knee. "Thank you, Sir," she whispered.

~*~

They explored the contents of Liam's refrigerator together. Bonnie had provided a loaf of sourdough bread, plenty of fruit, cold cuts and cheeses, milk, orange juice and several of her apparently famous casseroles, including chicken with pasta, ham with potato and broccoli and Liam's apparent favorite, an Irish shepherd's pie. Allie, whose refrigerator at home primarily contained bottles of ancient condiments and half-empty takeout containers, was suitably impressed.

Over a lunch of roast beef sandwiches and fresh peaches, by some mutual consent they kept the conversation light, more directed toward their respective careers and experiences in college than their fledging

BDSM relationship. This shift into vanilla territory was made easier for Allie since she'd pulled on a tank top and shorts from the clothing she'd brought with her.

While Liam was putting the dishes in the sink, Allie returned what food needed to go back into the refrigerator. As she placed the mustard in the door, she noticed a black velvet bag about nine inches long tucked just behind a jar of mayonnaise. Curious, she picked it up. "What's this?"

Liam turned from the sink, his lips lifting into a sexy smile when he saw what she was holding. "I was wondering if you'd notice that. I selected it especially for you from my collection. I moved it from the freezer to the fridge while you were putting on some clothes. We're going to use it this afternoon down in the dungeon."

Allie clutched the bag. There was something hard inside it. "Go on," Liam said. "Open it."

She untied the drawstring and cautiously slid the item from the bag onto her palm. Made of glass, it was shaped like a huge penis. Small, raised bumps covered the surface. Still wrapped in its original shrink-wrap, it was icy cold to the touch.

She looked up at Liam, who was watching her intently. "What is this?" she asked, "some kind of dildo?"

"That's precisely what it is."

Allie stared at the toy, at once repelled and fascinated. "Isn't this kind of dangerous? Couldn't it shatter or something?"

Liam shook his head. "It's made of a special kind of glass," he explained. "It's as solid as steel. You couldn't break it if you tried."

Allie slid the bumpy glass phallus back into its velvet bag, her vaginal muscles spasming with nervous anticipation as she imagined Liam inserting the thick, long sex toy inside her.

Liam was watching her, a slow, sensual smile moving over his face. He reached for his walking cane. "Let's go downstairs. I want to use you. Bring the velvet bag with you." He walked from the room, leaving Allie to follow him.

At the head of the basement stairs, he was waiting. "Take off your clothes," he instructed. "You will always be naked when you enter my dungeon."

Setting the velvet bag down carefully, Allie quickly shucked her clothing, leaving it in a little pile at the head of the stairs.

Sir Liam, watching her, instructed, "Bring the panties with you." He didn't explain why, and Allie didn't ask, though she was instantly curious.

As before, Sir Liam had her go down first. As she walked down the stairs, she toyed with the idea of "accidentally" dropping the velvet bag and letting it tumble down the stairs, though she knew even as this decidedly un-submissive thought flitted through her head, that the specially-made glass wouldn't shatter.

Once in the dungeon, Sir Liam took the velvet bag and the panties from Allie. He directed her to stand beneath a series of heavy ropes that had been tied over the rough-hewn beams affixed to the basement's ceiling. The end of each rope was knotted around a large metal ring.

Sir Liam went to a tall cabinet set against one wall. Opening it, he removed several items, along with a black duffel bag, into which he dropped his selections, including, she noted, the glass dildo in its velvet sack. When he returned to her, he set his walking cane and the duffel on the floor.

He had a pair of leather cuffs in his hands. "Hold out your wrists," he instructed. He placed the cuffs on her, securing them with two-sided metal clips. When he was done, he said, "Lift your arms over your head. See if you can grab the rings on the ends of those two ropes there." He pointed upward. Allie lifted her arms. She wasn't quite able to reach the rings.

Sir Liam, several inches taller than she, pulled at the ropes, lowering them until she could grab hold. As he clipped her cuffs to the rings, Allie's nipples tightened and engorged. Once she was secured, he tugged at the ropes, adjusting them until her arms were fully extended.

Sir Liam stood in front of her. "Spread your legs." As he spoke, he cupped her bare mons, causing a shudder of pure lust to quake through her frame. With a moan, she pushed against his hand.

Sir Liam smiled cruelly as he pulled his hand away. "Control yourself, sub girl."

Allie looked away, embarrassed that her lust had gotten the better of her. She

shifted her feet as directed, the change in position adding tension to the cuffs that held her wrists in place. Her heart was tapping like a hammer against her sternum. Something about being suspended in this position created an enormous sense of vulnerability.

Sir Liam bent down and reached into the duffel once more, withdrawing the velvet bag. He slipped the dildo from it and pulled off the protective wrapping. He held up the glass penis for Allie to see. "I'm going to fuck you with this, sub Allie," he said, his eyes hooding with lust.

Allie couldn't tear her eyes away from the enormous phallus. "Please, Sir," she said nervously. "I'm afraid. That thing looks too big."

Sir Liam only smiled. "A little fear is a good thing," he said. "As to its size, you don't need to worry. I have this." Reaching again into the duffel, he pulled out a small tube of lubricant. Flicking open its plastic top, he squeezed a healthy dollop over the head of the glass cock.

Allie jumped when the cold, gooey thing nudged between her legs.

Using his other hand, Sir Liam reached for the back of Allie's neck as he lowered his face to hers. "Trust me," he murmured, his lips brushing hers. Then he kissed her, his tongue slipping into her mouth as he pushed the icy cock slowly but surely into her cunt.

Allie grunted against the invasion of her sex, the phallus stretching her wide as Sir Liam continued to kiss her, his mouth hard on hers, his fingers twining in her hair. Keeping hold of the dildo, he began to move it. The little bumps along its sides tickled inside her. When he thrust it in a certain way, she gasped, a jolt of icy fire sending waves of pleasure through her. He thrust harder, the phallus moving like a cock, stroking her sweet spot as he kissed her mouth with rising passion until she began to tremble.

When he finally let her go, Allie gasped, still trembling. The dildo lodged in her cunt remained cold, but a fire blazed inside her soul. She wanted more. Her nipples ached and her clit throbbed.

Sir Liam regarded her with a knowing smile, his eyes glittering. "See that? I knew you could handle it."

Bending down, he produced Allie's panties from the duffel bag. Crouching in front of her, he said, "Step into these. They'll help keep the glass dildo in place for the rest of this session."

Allie obediently lifted one leg and then the other as Sir Liam slid the silky underwear up her thighs and settled it into place, pulling the elastic waistband high to add pressure to the base of the dildo nestled deep inside her.

He reached once more into the duffel, this time removing a slim, black butt plug covered in shrink-wrap. He held it up so Allie could see. "This vibrating butt plug should add an interesting dimension to your experience." He opened his other hand to reveal a small, oval remote control.

Though Allie was no stranger to butt plugs, they weren't her favorite things. Yet, aroused as she was, it didn't occur to her to protest. The concept of a vibrating plug was new to her and, actually, quite intriguing.

She watched with both eagerness and trepidation as Liam unwrapped the butt plug and lubricated its tip. He moved to stand behind her and pulled her panties aside. In spite of herself, Allie flinched when she felt what she assumed to be the plug make contact with her asshole.

"Relax," Sir Liam said soothingly. "It's just my finger for now." He moved his fingertip gently over the tiny, tight pucker. He pressed gently past her sphincter muscle. "Good," he said. "Now I'll add a second finger. You will remain open and relaxed to my touch."

"Yes, Sir," Allie said a little breathlessly. Sir Liam was gentle, and the sensation was pleasurable, especially juxtaposed against the thick phallus that completely filled her cunt.

After a while, he withdrew his fingers. Something fell to the ground in her peripheral vision. Turning, she saw Sir Liam had dropped a latex glove to the floor beside her. She forgot about this when she felt the insistent nudge of the butt plug between her cheeks.

"Stay in that place you were a moment ago," Sir Liam urged. "Don't tense up. Take what I'm giving you. Take what you need."

He slipped the plug past her sphincter, easing it in slowly. "Excellent," Sir Liam announced. "You took the whole thing. I knew you could do it." He moved once more to stand in front of her, the tiny remote in his hand. "How do you feel, sub Allie? What does it feel like to be filled in both holes, suspended by your wrists from the ceiling and completely at my mercy?"

The glass cock was still cold inside her, though her own internal heat had mitigated much of the chill. The dildo was thick and hard, and she could feel the pressure of the butt plug against it, separated only by the thin membranes of her body.

"It feels very full, Sir," she said, aware her description was lame. She tugged at the wrist cuffs that held her arms high overhead. "I feel especially vulnerable like this."

"Only vulnerable?" Sir Liam queried. "Nothing else?" He leaned down and closed his mouth over her left nipple, flicking his tongue over it and then biting down gently.

Allie moaned, her nipple pulsing in his teeth. Her cunt muscles spasmed against the glass cock. Suddenly, the butt plug embedded deep inside her whirred to life. Allie jumped, startled. Her nipple, still caught in Liam's teeth, received a painful tug.

Sir Liam let that nipple go and shifted his focus to her right nipple, which received the same sensual attention. When he stepped back, her nipples were red and shiny from his kisses. The vibrating butt plug made the phallus buried in her cunt vibrate as well, causing her clit to pulse with aching need.

Fuck me. Fuck me now!

"You want to be fucked, don't you?" Sir Liam said in a low voice, reading her mind.

"Yes," Allie breathed. "God, yes."

"In my dungeon, you have to earn your pleasure."

All at once, he gripped her throat, his forefinger and thumb digging into the soft flesh just below her jaw. His face was close, his brilliant green eyes locked on hers as he pressed hard, and harder still.

Allie was unable to draw a breath. Unable to move. Her heart thumped and squeezed in her chest, the blood roaring in her ears. Liam moved closer, their faces nearly touching. "I own you, sub Allie. Your very life is in my hands. You do understand that, don't you?"

Allie was unable even to nod her head. The pressure was building behind her face, and she thought she might pass out. Her eyelids began to flutter shut.

"Open your eyes," Sir Liam commanded, his voice hard. Allie forced her eyes to open. She saw the power and the lust in Sir Liam's face and real fear shot through her blood. She jerked hard in her bonds, trying desperately to pull away from his iron grip.

All at once, he let her go. Allie drew in a deep, ragged breath, and then another. "Oh my God," she gasped when she could finally speak. "You nearly choked me to death!"

Sir Liam only smiled. "Nowhere near to death, sub Allie. You panicked because you don't yet trust me. This is an exercise in trust. We will try it again." Without giving her a chance to reply, once again he reached for her throat, pinning her in place with his strong hand. "Keep your eyes locked on mine."

Allie struggled to do as he said, blinking rapidly to keep from closing her eyes. The vibrating plug and glass phallus inside her, along with the heightened awareness that her life truly was in this man's hands, had combined to create a fierce, persistent pulsing at her clit. Shit, was she going to come?

As if she'd spoken aloud, Sir Liam, tightening his grip on her throat, growled, "Don't even think about it."

A wave of dizziness assailed her, and Allie's head would have fallen back if Sir Liam's strong grip hadn't held her in place. "Keep your eyes on me," he reminded her. "I'm going to count to five. Then I will let you go." He began to count.

Allie could barely hear him over the pounding of her heart. "Three, four, five."

She sagged in her bonds as she sucked in a bushel full of air. She hung limply in her cuffs, as if the bones had dissolved in her body. Sweat was drying on her skin, though at the same time she was shivery, not with cold, but with desire. She wasn't crying, yet tears were streaming down her cheeks.

Sir Liam brushed them away with his thumbs. "You're doing really well, sub Allie. You're almost there. You've got a lot of walls erected between you and the complete submission you crave. I will help you break down those walls. I want to continue with this exercise."

He stepped back, regarding her. "If you can't speak at any point, you will hold up your index finger like this." He demonstrated the gesture. "Unless you use your safeword or make that signal, we will continue."

Allie lifted her head and met Sir Liam's gaze. She was both afraid and exhilarated, as if she were perched on the edge of the cliff, spreading wings for the first time, ready to soar. "Yes, Sir Liam. I understand," she said, her voice hoarse.

"You please me."

His words moved through her like warm, powerful liquor. She found the strength to stand upright, the bones of her skeleton reforming inside her, even as the resolve stiffened in her soul. She drew in a deep breath, and then his hand was on her throat once more, immediately cutting off her ability to breathe.

"Keep your eyes on mine," Sir Liam reminded her once more as he held her captive in his viselike grip. "This time, I will count to twenty. You will focus on surrender. You will not think about the fact that you cannot breathe. You will give yourself completely to me, not considering the consequences but focusing only on trust in your Master."

Once again, he began to count. Allie tried to do as he said, but by the count of ten she could feel the panic rising in her gut, a spurt of adrenaline heating her blood.

"Focus," Sir Liam interrupted himself to say. "Trust me. Trust yourself."

A strange thought floated into Allie's mind, barely perceived amidst the roil of panic. The thought was persistent enough that it did eventually penetrate her understanding.

You belong to Sir Liam. Sir Liam will take you where you need to go. Sir Liam will keep you safe.

He was still holding her just as tightly as before, his counting slow and steady. But something changed inside Allie. Her muscles, bunched and tensed a moment before, began to loosen. The panic that had balled into a fist in her gut dissolved. She became aware, once more, of the intense, vibrating pleasure in her ass and sex, but her primary focus was on Sir Liam's deep, emerald green eyes, which gripped her as surely as his hand.

"Twenty."

Allie was vaguely aware he had reached the magic number, but he didn't release his hold on her throat. Instead, he breathed, "Yes. Yes, that's it. Surrender to me."

Allie didn't panic as a blanket of warm, black velvet draped itself over her senses. She wrapped herself in its serenity and drifted peacefully away.

CHAPTER 7

The next morning when Allie woke up, her hand was between her legs, her fingers moving rapidly over her swollen clit. Erotic dreams involving whips, rope and Sir Liam still swirled through her mind, more real than the bed she lay in or the man beside her.

As she came more fully awake, she yanked her hand away, Sir Liam's admonition about masturbation returning to her. She turned her head, holding her breath as she peered at her new lover, afraid he might have been aware of her indiscretion and was, even now, waiting to punish her.

Liam, however, appeared dead to the world, his eyes closed, a small comforting snore issuing from his slightly open mouth. As she had the morning before, Allie turned onto her side and lifted herself on her elbow to regard him more carefully. "Liam," she whispered, testing how deeply he slept. He didn't stir. She placed her hand lightly on his shoulder. He closed his mouth and swallowed, but otherwise didn't move.

Emboldened, she moved her hand slowly down his abdomen. His skin was warm and supple and he smelled faintly of fresh bread, sandalwood soap and sleep. Her fingers stopped at the thin fabric of his pajama pants. She understood without his saying that he was embarrassed about his lame leg. At the same time, it seemed a little ridiculous, especially after the intensely intimate sessions they'd shared, not only in the dungeon, but in this very bed, that he should keep himself covered in this way.

Without consciously making the decision, Allie slipped her fingers beneath the loose elastic of his pajama pants. She remained motionless for several seconds, but Liam did not react. Slowly, carefully, she eased the pants down until his morning erection was revealed in all its splendor. Her mouth instantly watering, Allie pondered if she dared to suck her Master's cock without his express permission. Deciding to take the risk, she shimmied quietly down until she was in position to lower her head and close her lips over the head of his shaft.

Liam moaned. Allie paused, waiting for a cue to stop or continue. After a moment, Liam's hand touched the back of her head, exerting a gentle pressure. Grinning around his cock, Allie went to work with enthusiasm to please her man. His breath quickened as she licked and sucked his hard, smooth shaft, using her free hand to stroke his balls. His skin grew hot, the vein along his cock throbbing against her tongue. It wasn't long before his body stiffened suddenly, and with a soft cry, he spurted into her mouth. Allie eagerly swallowed every drop.

Liam's hand fell away from the back of her head. She stayed as she was, his cock still in her mouth. She expected Liam to do or say something, but he lay still and quiet, his breath slowly deepening as his shaft softened. Had he fallen back asleep? Had he ever really been awake?

Allie let his cock slip from between her lips and slowly lifted her head to regard his face. His eyes were closed, a small smile on his lips. Allie looked from his face to his body. The sheets had fallen away, and his pajama bottoms were pushed to mid thigh. On his left leg she saw the beginning of a dark red, ridged scar. She glanced at his face. He appeared once more deeply asleep.

Looking back down at his leg, she silently slipped her fingers beneath the elastic of his pajama pants. She tugged them gently down his legs, fully revealing his thighs to the knees.

Tears of compassion came to her eyes as she stared at the roadmap of angry, ridged scars that crisscrossed his left thigh. His left leg was markedly thinner than the right, as if the muscle had been torn from the bone. She could only imagine what he'd been through, both in being involved in such an obviously horrific accident, and in the year following as he struggled to recover and reclaim his life. Cautiously, she touched one of the scars, the red skin smooth and hot beneath her fingers.

In a sudden flurry of motion, Liam jerked away with a cry. He pushed her away with one hand while yanking at his pajamas with the other. "What the hell," he shouted. "What the hell do you think you're doing?"

Startled, Allie jerked her head to look at his face. A dark flush was moving up his throat and cheeks, his eyes narrowed in genuine anger. "What?" she cried, disconcerted by his strong reaction. "Liam, what is it? Did I hurt you?"

All at once the anger drained from his face. He fell back against the pillows, covering his face with his forearm. "I'm sorry, Allie," he said. "You startled me, is all." He sounded miserable and Allie wished she could rewind the last ten minutes.

Not sure what to do, she waited for him to say more, to look at her, to do something. When he didn't, she said quietly, more as a statement than a question. "That's not all, is it?"

Liam didn't move, but after several beats, he said, "No, that's not all. The truth is I didn't want you to see my leg. I didn't want you to think less of me."

Allie could sense the shame and the pain in his words and her heart squeezed with pity and love. She lay down beside him and rested her cheek on his chest. "Liam," she said softly, "I'm so sorry for what happened to you. Surely you know you couldn't keep that from me forever, but I'm sorry I looked before you were ready to show me. That was wrong of me."

Liam said nothing to this, but some of his tension seemed to ease. She wrapped her arm around him.

"I think your scars are beautiful," she whispered.

Liam snorted at this, as Allie had expected he might.

"I'm serious," she persisted. "They're beautiful because they represent how you fought your way back from a traumatic situation that must have been horrible, both physically and emotionally. I see the damage that's been done to your muscles, and I'm guessing to your bones as well." She lifted her head. "Was the leg broken?"

Finally, Liam lowered his arm and Allie shifted so she could see his face. "Yeah. In eight places," he replied. "The doctors told me I'd never be able to walk on the leg again, but I refused to listen. I've got enough metal in there now that I'll set off the machines at the airport if I ever travel again." He managed a small laugh. "Three surgeries, multiple skin grafts, months of physical therapy at the rehab clinic. I'm still doing PT, though I mostly do that myself now."

"You see that?" Allie persisted, determined to help him see his own strength. "A lesser man might have given up. A lesser man might have succumbed to self-pity instead of fighting his way back to a full life. I have to tell you, Liam, I am in awe."

Liam smiled, though his eyes remained troubled. "Thanks, Allie. That means a lot." Turning toward her, he ran two fingers gently along her cheek. "I'm sorry. I should have trusted you. I ask you to trust me as your Dom, but I wasn't willing to do the same with you. I guess"—he paused, as if gathering his thoughts—"I guess I was afraid to risk ruining what we had." He smiled ruefully. "It's easy to be a strong Dom online and on the phone. It's real life that can be so goddamned messy. I knew eventually you would have to see my leg, but I kept thinking we had time."

Allie lifted herself to her knees on the mattress beside Liam. She brought her arms behind her head and laced her fingers against her neck. "Sir Liam, we do have time. All the time we need. I am so honored to be your sub girl. I am ready to continue in our exploration of intensity and passion. Please allow me to serve you, Sir, in whatever way pleases you."

At her words, something returned to his face—that sense of confident power that had so drawn her to him in the first place. "Sub Allie," he replied, his natural dominance reasserting itself, "thank you for the gift of your submission. I look forward to continuing our exploration as well. I'd say today is a good day to push a few boundaries."

A rush of excited anticipation shot through Allie's frame, her nipples leaping to instant attention at the thought of another intense session in the dungeon. Sir Liam's tone lightened. "But first, shower and breakfast."

He slung his legs over the side of the bed, gripped his cane and stood. He kicked his pajama bottoms away, and Allie had a lovely view of his small, muscular ass. He glanced at her over his shoulder. "Coming?"

"Yes, Sir." Allie scampered off the bed and followed Liam to the bathroom. He gestured for her to use the toilet first, while he turned on the hot water for the shower. Once they had brushed their teeth, they moved into the stall together.

They stood beneath the water, their arms locked around each other. Allie lifted her face so her mouth nearly reached Liam's ear. "Does it hurt?" she asked, reaching down to run her fingers lightly over the ridged scars on his left thigh. "Does it hurt all the time?"

Liam reached for her hand, taking it in his. "Pretty much, yeah. But you learn to deal with it. Sometimes it's worse than other times. I try to harness the pain, to use it to remind me that I'm still here. I'm still alive."

It seemed as if he was going to say something else, to add more, but instead, he lowered his face to hers and kissed her as the water cascaded over them. Allie forgot everything but his mouth on hers, his hands moving sensually over her body.

"I had this fantastic dream this morning," Liam said as they stepped apart. "It had to be a dream, since no sub girl of mine would dare to worship her Master's cock without permission, eh?"

Allie drew in a breath and studied Liam's face. Was he going to punish her? But his eyes were dancing, and he smiled as he added, "Free pass this one time, sub girl. But from this point forward, you don't take such liberties, are we clear?"

"Yes, Sir," Allie whispered, aware she'd gotten off easier than she deserved. "Thank you, Sir."

After they washed up, Liam stepped out of the stall first. "There's a new razor there on the ledge for you. You may groom yourself while I get some breakfast going. You will remain naked today, as that pleases me."

When Allie entered the kitchen, Liam was just taking something out of the oven. Dressed in jeans, he was shirtless, his feet bare. "Can I help with anything, Sir?" she asked, drinking in his sexy, hairy chest with her eyes.

"Sure, you can get the coffee carafe and the mugs and put them on the table. There's cream in the refrigerator. If you could get that and the butter and jam, that would be perfect."

While Allie brought things to the table, Liam dumped the steaming biscuits into a large wicker basket lined with a cloth napkin. "That smells fantastic," Allie enthused, her stomach rumbling. "Another gift from Bonnie?"

Liam shook his head. "No, I actually made these myself. I find that baking relaxes me. I like to make bread. I make these in advance and freeze them. Then I just pull out what I need."

"Impressive," Allie said, for a moment slipping out of sub mode. "I make a mean Lean Cuisine in the microwave," she joked, though in fact that was about the extent of her cooking repertoire. As Liam chuckled, she pulled out a chair at the table, intending to sit down.

"No," he said, placing his hand on the chair to stop her. "This morning, you will kneel on a cushion beside me. You will place your hands behind your back and I will feed you."

Allie hesitated a moment, recalling a bad memory involving a prior boyfriend with a special fondness for squirting Hershey's Syrup and whipped cream over various parts of her body as a prelude to very sticky, not very enjoyable sex. Reminding herself Sir Liam was nothing like that guy, she lowered herself to the cushion and clasped her arms behind her back.

She watched hungrily as Liam split a hot biscuit and placed a pat of butter on one half. He added some apricot jam and then put the second half of the biscuit on top of the first. He cut the biscuit into bite-size pieces. Selecting one of the pieces, he held it between forefinger and thumb. "Open your mouth and stick out your tongue," he instructed her.

Allie, starving now, eagerly obeyed. Liam set the morsel on her tongue, and Allie chewed the delicious, flaky biscuit, savoring the melted butter and sweet tang of the jam against the perfectly cooked bread. Liam prepared another biscuit and lifted it to his mouth, taking a large bite. As he ate, he poured two mugs of coffee. Having apparently paid attention, he made Allie's just the way she liked it, with plenty of cream and one teaspoon of sugar. Finally, he offered her a second bite of biscuit, which she eagerly accepted, followed by several sips of hot, strong coffee.

Allie, used to gobbling her food, was forced to wait patiently as Liam doled out her breakfast, one bite at a time, while also eating his own. It was a new experience for her, and if not precisely erotic, it was clearly a lesson in giving up control. To her surprise, she quite liked being fed in this way. She liked when he wiped the corner of her mouth with his napkin, and the way he carefully held the rim of the mug to her lips. She felt cared for in a way she hadn't experienced since she was a child.

When they had both eaten their fill and finished their coffee, Sir Liam pushed back from the table and reached for his walking cane. "We can clean this up later. Come on. It's time to go to the dungeon now." He headed out of the kitchen, and Allie followed. This time he went down the stairs first, allowing Allie to see his uneven, swinging gait. This, she understood, was an act of trust on his part, and the realization moved her.

He led her to the beautifully constructed St. Andrew's cross. "I've never seen such a pretty cross, Sir." Allie ran her finger over the silvery steel set in the wood, admiring the simple, elegant design.

The pride evident on his face, Sir Liam said, "It's cool, right? I had it custom-built by a friend of mine who makes BDSM furniture."

"Matt?" Allie asked, intrigued.

Sir Liam shook his head. "No, another friend. I haven't seen him in a long time." He brought his hand to his forehead and pushed back his hair, a thoughtful look on his face. "I guess I really haven't seen anyone for a long time. Maybe it's time for that to change."

Allie said nothing to this, although she understood it was some kind of turning point for her new lover. She wondered if her being here was in part responsible, and the thought pleased her.

She forgot her musings as Sir Liam said, "Stand with your back to the cross, and lift your arms against the top of the X." Allie obeyed, a shivery wash of erotic anticipation moving over her skin as Sir Liam buckled her wrists into the leather cuffs secured to the cross, then squatted to bind her ankles in the same fashion. As always happened when she was bound, a buttery, delicious sensation of release moved through her body, while at the same time, her clit and nipples hardened with erotic anticipation.

Apparently satisfied she was properly restrained, Sir Liam moved temporarily out of her line of vision. When he returned, he carried a tripod in one hand, a long, white wand with a huge baton-like round head in the other. She knew immediately what it was, though this one had no cord.

No, no, no, no. Absolutely not. Somehow she managed to hold her tongue for the moment, but she'd have to say something. *You're supposed to say something. Communication is paramount, remember?*

Sir Liam set down the tripod directly in front of Allie. Looking at her and then the apparatus, he adjusted the height of the thing until he was satisfied. When he straightened, Allie burst out, "Is that one of those Hitachi Wand things?"

"It is," Sir Liam agreed calmly. "Is there a problem, sub Allie? Something you need to discuss with me? You may speak freely."

More unwelcome memories of yet another boyfriend in yet another failed relationship assailed her, but she shook them away. Sir Liam was different. He would listen. He would really hear her.

"Thank you, Sir." Allie blew out a breath, trying to think how to phrase her concerns without coming across like a willful brat. "It's just that, um, I had a kind of bad experience with one of those things during a scene. They're too intense for me; too powerful," she added nervously.

"Thank you for letting me know your concerns, sub Allie. I will certainly take them into consideration during this exercise."

"Thank you, Sir." Allie knew it was too much to hope that he abandon his plans. She silently counseled herself to trust the man who so far hadn't missed a step in their new and exciting BDSM dance. She watched as he secured the wand into place on the tripod, though, to her relief, he moved it to one side so he could stand directly in front of her.

"I'm sorry you had a bad experience with the wand. It sounds like whoever was using it didn't really know what they were doing. I do, however." He let that sink in a moment and then added, "Regarding the intensity, let me set your mind at rest. First of all"—reaching over, he touched a dial on the side of the wand and the fat head began to vibrate ominously—"this deluxe model has an adjustable control, so I can very precisely calibrate the level of stimulation." He turned the dial again and the vibrator stilled. "That said, I don't expect you to climax. In fact, I forbid it. If I think you're about to come, I will do this to get your attention."

All at once, he slapped her across the face with his open hand. Allie gasped in shock and instinctively jerked her head away. He slapped the other cheek just as hard.

"Sir," Allie cried breathlessly. "You're scaring me." Her cheeks tingled and stung, but at the same time she couldn't deny the sudden flame of desire that had ignited deep in her loins.

"You need to calm yourself. Draw from your inner strength. Trust me, sub Allie. I won't take you anywhere unsafe." Allie relaxed a little at his words, though she still didn't entirely understand her own powerful, confused reactions. As if Sir Liam could see directly into her mind, he offered, "It's clear you have a strong emotional response to face slapping. It both frightens and excites you, am I right?"

Confused but unwilling to lie, Allie nodded. "Yes, Sir, though I don't understand it."

"It's one of those delicious dichotomies a submissive masochist experiences—genuine fear coupled with fierce desire—a very potent combination when handled correctly."

He gently stroked the cheek he'd just slapped. "Face slapping can trigger unpleasant feelings and memories. And, especially when you're bound as you are now, helpless and defenseless, it serves to heighten the uneven balance of power between us." His voice softened, though Allie could sense the steel of his resolve. "This is where the trust comes in, sub Allie. For this session, I'm going to sexually stimulate you with the wand, while at the same time slapping your face to keep you focused.

"You need to feel free to tell me what is happening with you. In fact, I insist on it. I know you seek the intensity this experience will offer you, but I also acknowledge this is a trigger for you. So if you need me to stop, just use your safeword, and I'll stop. That said, I want you to give this a chance. Open your mind and your body to what I'm offering you. If you can, try to let go of previously held fears and preconceived notions of what you can and can't handle. You don't need those anymore. They no longer serve you."

He took her face in both hands then and dipped his head, gently kissing her mouth. When he let her go, he stepped back, his eyes fixed on her face. "It's your decision, sub Allie. If you tell me this exercise is too much for you even to try, we can stop now. But if you can find the courage to continue, I promise it will be an experience you won't soon forget." He tucked a strand of her unruly hair behind one ear. "So, I will ask you now, are you ready to experience the vibrating wand and the sting of my palm, sub Allie?"

Allie's focus shifted from Sir Liam's face to the ominous wand waiting for her in the tripod. She looked at his large, masculine hands, her cheeks still tingling, though the sting had faded. So far, every step of the way with this man, every time she had trusted him, he had rewarded her trust with new and increasingly intense experiences, all of which had fed her starved submissive soul.

She met his eyes, willing the strength of her resolve to override the fear. "Yes, Sir. As ready as I can be."

Sir Liam smiled. "Fair enough. Then we begin." Reaching into his jeans pocket, he pulled out a small tube of lubricant. This he squirted over the head of the Hitachi wand. He moved the tripod until it was directly in front of her, edging it closer until the gooey head of the vibrator pressed against Allie's smooth mons. He spread her pussy lips, pushing the wand head gently until it was firmly lodged against her clit. Stepping back, he touched the dial on the side of the wand.

The pulse was admittedly far gentler than what she'd experienced in the past. It didn't hurt, but it tickled. Allie squirmed, but she was unable to move away from the wand's persistent vibration. Sir Liam touched the dial again, and the wand hummed louder, vibrating more insistently against her clit. The tickling shifted to something less annoying, perhaps even slightly pleasurable.

He stroked the dial again, and a jolt of hot pleasure shot suddenly through Allie's loins. "Oh," she gasped involuntarily. The spiral of shuddery pleasure continued to unwind inside her.

As suddenly as before, Sir Liam's hand came up, striking her cheek with a stinging blow. "Focus. Control yourself." He slapped her other cheek.

Allie jerked back, emitting a startled cry, the pleasure at her sex diminished by the shock. Yet, she had to admit, she was wildly aroused. The sharp points of panic the face slapping had poked into her pleasure were mitigated by the undeniable sexual thrill of her position and the situation. She was in this sexy, powerful man's dungeon, tethered against his cross, arms and legs spread wide, a vibrator throbbing at her cunt, her face stinging from his hand. She was dizzy, and when she tried to take in a breath, her lungs refused to fill. She realized she was panting.

"Breathe," Sir Liam reminded her, his tone soothing. "Slow down. Show me you can do this."

Allie struggled to obey, sucking in what air she could and releasing it slowly. As her head began to clear, Sir Liam touched the dial again, and the vibrator kicked up its intensity. "Oooooh," Allie moaned, the syllable held for several seconds as she struggled to regain control. As impossible as it seemed, her body was signaling an impending orgasm.

Again he slapped her, hard across her left cheek and then her right, giving her no chance to anticipate or recover. "No!" Allie cried before she could stop herself. "I can't!" The vibrator continued to thrum between her legs. Her cheeks were flaming, her body trembling. She would have fallen if the cuffs hadn't held her in place.

Sir Liam stepped back at once, pulling the vibrator back so it no longer touched her throbbing sex. "I don't hear your safeword. Are you ending this session? Or are you just reacting off your fear, instead of pushing through it, instead of embracing it?"

Allie swallowed hard. She did feel especially vulnerable, the face slapping heightening her helplessness. At the same time she couldn't deny how incredibly turned on she was. Sir Liam was watching her intently, clearly waiting for her response. "I don't know, Sir," she answered honestly. "I'm not entirely sure what I'm feeling."

"Would you like me to help you sort out those feelings?"

"Yes, please."

"I'll tell you what I think. I think you can do this. More than that, I think you want to do this. You want to see where this exercise will take you. You're afraid, but at the same time you're excited." Allie couldn't deny what he was saying. She nodded in mute agreement. Sir Liam continued, "Would you like to hand the decision to me? Are you able to trust me to read your body and your reactions, to gauge what you can and can't handle?"

An undeniable surge of relief washed through Allie. She would give herself over to Sir Liam, to her Master. She would trust him. "Yes, please, Sir. Thank you, Sir."

With a nod, Sir Liam returned the tripod to its position and adjusted the wand until the head was once more firmly nestled between her labia. He eased the dial slowly, giving her time to adjust to the increasing intensity. As the pleasure quickly mounted, she struggled to keep her body under control. She began to tremble again, sweat breaking out over her skin, her breath once more a ragged pant.

Just when she knew she was going to lose the battle, Sir Liam slapped her face, jerking her out of the sexual swoon that had nearly pulled her under. He slapped her several more times, alternating cheeks as she squeezed her eyes closed and tried to keep her rising panic at bay.

"Look at me," he commanded, though she could barely hear him over the pounding of her heart. "Let me see your eyes. Focus on my face."

Allie struggled to obey. Her cheeks were on fire. Her clit felt swollen to the size of a cherry, her cunt aching to be filled.

He eased the dial up a notch and then slapped her again. Allie uttered a low, primal moan, her entire body trembling uncontrollably, tears slipping down her hot cheeks. He slapped her again and again, until the oddest thing began to happen. Somehow her spirit seemed to slip from her body. It rose and hovered just above her, watching as she trembled, shuddered and jerked, overloaded by the relentless touch of the wand and the sharp clap of Sir Liam's palm.

"Oh, god!" she heard herself cry, her voice rising to a high-pitched whine. "Oh, god, help me, help me!"

Even as the words left her mouth, she had no idea what she was asking for help with, but Sir Liam must have understood because he said, "I am helping you. I'm helping you get where you need to go. And now you have permission. Come for me, sub Allie. Give yourself over to the sensations. Do it. Now."

He slapped her once more and then stepped back, letting the vibrating wand lift her into a sphere that was new to her. Her spirit slipped back into her body as she was hurled and tumbled under waves of orgasmic pleasure the likes of which she'd never experienced in her life. At first she struggled against the onslaught of such intense, blinding sensation, but at last she gave in, letting its undertow drag her down, down, down…

She opened her eyes, for a moment completely confused, with no idea where she was or how she got there. Liam was gazing tenderly down at her, cradling her in his arms. He was seated on the floor of the dungeon, leaning against the St. Andrew's cross.

"Gosh," Allie said, smiling weakly, "I feel like I left the planet. I didn't know it was even *possible* to experience something so intense. It was fucking *amazing*," she added, awestruck as the memory of the most powerful orgasm of her life returned to her. She was lying across Liam's lap, supported by a strong arm around her shoulders. "I guess I must have passed out or something."

"Or something," Liam agreed, returning her smile.

CHAPTER 8

A few days later they walked down the aisle at the Home Depot not far from Liam's neighborhood. The unseasonably cool and rainy spring day worked well for Liam's purposes, as it enabled him to carry out his plans more easily.

Allie, walking beside him, was wearing one of his windbreakers draped loosely over her shoulders. To the casual passerby, she appeared simply to have her hands clasped behind her back beneath the jacket. In fact, her wrists were cuffed in leather and clipped together. She had a slim anal plug in her ass and a Venus butterfly vibrator strapped in place beneath her short skirt. She wore neither bra nor panties.

Liam fingered the small remote in his pocket as they approached his favorite aisle. He smiled as Allie's eyes widened, her lips lightly parting as she took in the huge reels of chain and rope arrayed on shelf after shelf. He touched the remote, bringing the vibrator to life.

"Oh!" Allie exclaimed softly as the soft rubbery body of the butterfly thrummed against her clit.

"Remember," Liam reminded her, putting his hand on her shoulder for emphasis, "you are not to orgasm. No matter what."

Allie met his gaze. "No, Sir. I won't."

They stopped in front of a reel of chain with one-inch links. Liam reached for the end of the chain and slowly unwound several feet. Using the chain cutter provided by the store, he clipped about six feet and looped it around his arm.

"I'm going to use this on you this afternoon when we get home," he informed Allie. "I'm going to chain you to the wall in the water play area. After I tease and torture you with the water hose, I'll place you in the submersion tub for an intense exercise in trust and obedience."

As he spoke, he upped the intensity of vibration at Allie's sex until she shuddered and bit her lip, probably to keep from moaning aloud. Liam's cock hardened as he watched her.

A shopping cart suddenly appeared from around the corner of the aisle. It was moving very quickly, though Liam couldn't see anyone pushing it. The cart suddenly rushed towards them with no signs of slowing. Instinctively, Liam pushed Allie to the side, shielding her body with his. As a result, the corner of the oncoming cart caught him hard, ramming directly into his left leg.

Burning pain ripped through him like a hot knife. "Ah," he cried, jerking away from the cart, both the coiled chain on his arm and his walking cane clattering to the ground.

"Liam," Allie cried, "You're hurt!"

In spite of the pain, Liam managed to put his hand in his pocket to shut off the butterfly remote. "I'm okay," he managed through gritted teeth as sweat broke out on his forehead and upper lip.

A harried-looking woman appeared a moment later, shouting, "Jason, get back here with that cart right this second, you little shit." The mother barely glanced at Allie and Liam as she took off after the boy, who was rapidly disappearing around the corner.

Allie leaned into Liam. "She didn't even apologize," she said angrily.

"We should tell the manager."

"No, no, really, Allie, it's okay," Liam repeated. Angling away from her, he reached into his back pocket and pulled out the pill container he always carried with him. He dropped two of the tiny pills into his palm and popped them discreetly into his mouth. As he re-pocketed the container, he glanced down at the chain and his cane lying on the floor in front of them.

Allie, following his gaze, gave a small shrug. "Sorry. Wish I could pick those up for you, but I'm a bit tied up at the moment, ha ha. Now, if you wanted to remove the cuffs..." She lifted and dropped her shoulders beneath the windbreaker.

"Nah," Liam smiled, control returning to him. "I enjoy you like that too much to let you go." He bent and snagged the wrist strap on his cane, pulling it upright. Using the cane for support, he bent again and gathered up the length of chain. "Let's get out of here."

As they walked toward the front of the store, he reached into the pocket that held the remote and clicked it back on. Allie startled as the butterfly vibrated to life. "Remember," he said softly, bending down to murmur in her ear, "don't come, sub girl."

Back at the house, Liam had taken off Allie's wrist cuffs and allowed her to remove the butterfly and anal plug. "Take off the clothes, too," he had said. "You will have lunch naked and on your knees today."

After lunch, he brought her to the dungeon. He had her carry the chain they'd bought down the stairs as he led her to the water play area. After directing her to stand against the wall, Liam moved to the nearby supply cabinet. He selected a chain-link dog collar with a clip already in place on the leash ring, and an elastic hair tie. Returning to Allie, he gathered her shiny, coppery hair and twisted it into a ponytail to keep it off her face and neck, slipping the elastic over it to hold it in place. Gesturing for her to dip her head, he positioned the choke collar around her neck and adjusted it so it was snug but not too tight against her throat.

Taking the chain from her, he clipped one end to the collar and let the heavy links hang between her breasts. She sighed softly, her eyes shining with excitement and desire. Liam's cock tingled in response, dominance rising like a powerful beast inside him.

He stood in front of his beautiful sub girl. "Are you ready to submit to me today, sub Allie?"

"Yes, Sir." Her blue eyes were wide, her nipples erect.

"I'm going to use the hose. The water will be cold, its stream intense. I will both torture and pleasure you." Retrieving the stepstool from its place beside the submersion tub, he climbed it to attach the other end of the chain to a hook embedded in the wall for the purpose.

Stepping down, Liam admired the curve of her high, round breasts. Her nipples were distended and engorged with blood. Unable to resist, Liam reached for them, rolling and squeezing them until Allie winced. Her nipples still caught in his grip, he continued, "For this exercise I'm not going to bind you, other than this symbolic chain around your throat. You will raise your arms and place your hands behind your head. You will maintain that position, unless or until I tell you otherwise. You will stand with your legs spread wide, your pelvis tilted forward so that I have access to that sweet cunt of yours. You will not pull away from the water stream and you will not come, no matter how much I stimulate you. Are we crystal clear on this, sub Allie?" Releasing her nipples, he stepped back.

Allie swallowed hard and blinked several times, as if gathering her submissive courage. She looked both nervous and eager.

"Answer the question, sub girl," Liam said sternly. He reached between her legs and pressed a finger into her hot, wet cunt.

Allie gasped, but managed to reply, "Yes, Sir Liam. We are clear."

Satisfied, Liam went over to the hose that was hung over a large hook nearby. He unwound the hose and placed his finger on the nozzle's trigger. He turned the splitter on the faucet so the water would run out of the spigot not attached to the hose, in order to adjust the temperature. He placed his hand beneath the running water. Icy cold. He turned on the hot tap just enough so the temperature would keep her alert, without freezing her to death. Finally, he turned the splitter so the water would spray from the nozzle.

Stepping back, he adjusted the nozzle to a soft spray and aimed it in Allie's direction.

She squeezed her eyes closed.

"Open your eyes," he directed. "I want you fully present." He waited a moment as Allie complied. Then he pressed the trigger, directing the water against Allie's legs as he gave her a chance to adjust to its temperature and intensity.

"Oh, it's cold, Sir," she said, dancing on her toes as the water hit her thighs.

"It could be a lot colder," Liam advised. "If this were a punishment, rather than an exercise, I wouldn't have added any hot water. Now, stop dancing and stay still. Spread your legs wider and thrust your pelvis forward. Keep your back arched."

Allie shifted as directed, her eyes fixed on the hose, her hands behind her head. Liam aimed the nozzle upward, skirting past her smooth mons to let the water play against her breasts. Goose bumps rose on her flesh as he soaked her body and limbs with the cold spray. He aimed the stream for one nipple and then the other as Allie shuddered and sighed.

Satisfied she was ready for the next level, Liam adjusted the nozzle for a stronger spray and aimed it toward her sex.

Allie gave a small yelp as the water pummeled her pussy.

"Stay still," Liam reminded her. Aware of the power of reverse psychology, he added deviously, "And remember, do *not* come."

Allie had only orgasmed once in Liam's presence, as far as he knew, when the Hitachi wand had given her no choice in the matter. Since then, though they'd made love on multiple occasions, and while she'd certainly seemed to enjoy herself, she hadn't come. But neither had she faked it, and that was the important thing.

Feeling his power, Liam commanded, "Step forward from the wall until I tell you to stop." He watched as Allie inched carefully forward, her eyes widening as the choke chain tightened around her throat. "Okay, good," he said. "Now you may lower your arms. I want you to spread your pussy lips with your fingers and angle yourself so your clit is fully exposed to the spray. I want you to hold that position while I torture you with the water."

Allie hesitated for several seconds before obeying. Liam was about to reprimand her when she lowered her arms and assumed the position, revealing the red, swollen folds of her pretty sex and the small marble of a clit at the center. Liam moved a step closer, aiming the full force of the water at her spread pussy.

Allie moaned and began to squirm.

"Stay still," Liam admonished sharply. "Offer yourself to me. Prove you're willing to suffer for me." He moved the spray in small circles, letting the water cascade over her clit and labia.

Her body trembling, Allie cried, "Oh, god. I'm going to—"

"No, sub Allie," Liam said firmly. "You. Will. Not. Come." To give her a little relief, he moved the spray slightly downward so it didn't directly target her clit.

Allie's hands slipped as the water hit her right knuckle.

"Get back in position," Liam barked sharply. "I didn't tell you to move." Lowering the hose a moment, he waited until she had properly spread her cunt as directed. He pressed the trigger, aiming the water at her breasts and then moving it down her abdomen and along each thigh.

Finally he focused again on her dripping, reddened cunt. After only thirty seconds or so, she chanted her litany once more: *oh, god, oh, god, oh, god…* She was shaking, he suspected, not only because of an impending orgasm, but because she was cold. Deciding she had had enough, and not prepared to let her climax, Liam released the trigger.

"You may drop your hands to your sides," he said. He hung the hose haphazardly over the hook, making a mental note to coil it later. He reached quickly for a large bath towel from the stack he had at the ready nearby. This he wrapped around Allie's shoulders, allowing her to take hold of the towel as she shivered in its warm folds.

He released the chain and removed the choke collar. "You did reasonably well during the first part of this exercise," he said. "You had trouble controlling your body, but you did manage to do it with a little help and a few reminders."

Allie look down, as if embarrassed.

"Look at me," Liam directed. "This is a new situation for you, isn't it? Instead of having to fake an orgasm, you are learning to resist it. Quite a change in such a short time, wouldn't you agree?"

A look of wonderment crossed Allie's features, followed by a sudden mischievous smile. "It is a change, Sir. And, you know, I'd really like to finish what you started with the water, Sir. I would love to come, if that was possible, Sir."

Liam laughed as he shook his head. "It's nice to know what you would like, but, no, that most definitely is not possible, you sweet little slut. Remember, you have to earn it."

Placing an arm around her shoulders, Liam led Allie to the submersion tub, trying to put as little of his weight as possible on her as they moved. "The next part of this water exercise involves trust and courage. I'm going to bind your arms in front of you. Then you will sit in the tub and when I tap your shoulder, you will lie down in the water until your head and face are fully submerged. When I tap your shoulder again, you will rise. The exercise itself is simple. Executing it with grace and submission is not. Any question so far?"

"Is the water as cold as that spray was?" To emphasize her point, Allie gripped the towel, pulling it closer around her body.

"It's a good question, and no, you'll find this quite comfortable. It's heated to the temperature of a warm bath—about one hundred degrees."

He left her for a moment, moving toward the wall where he kept his rope collection. He selected several coils of thin, soft nylon rope that was easy to unknot quickly. Returning to Allie, he instructed her to cross her wrists at her waist. He wrapped the rope snuggly around her wrists and wound it between her legs so she felt its grip along her cunt and between her ass cheeks. Bringing the remaining length around her waist, he knotted it in place. Next, he wrapped her breasts in a crisscross pattern, not so tight that they would turn purple, but more to highlight them as an offering.

He stepped back to admire his handiwork. Was there anything sexier than a lovely woman naked and bound in rope? Her eyes were shining with anticipation, a softness to her features that he now recognized was brought on by the bondage.

"Your safeword gesture for this exercise will be the bending of your right knee so that it comes out of the water. If I do my job correctly, you won't need to use this gesture. I'm experienced in this kind of water play. You can actually hold your breath quite a bit longer than you think. I will assist you by covering your nose and mouth with my hand once you are submerged."

He placed his hands on Allie's shoulders and looked deep into her eyes. "How are you feeling right now?"

"Nervous," she answered quickly and then, after a pause, "and excited. Empowered. I'm scared, but I feel strong at the same time. Does that even make sense?"

"It makes perfect sense. Bravery only comes into play when we are afraid. The fear, for you, helps you focus. The bondage provides an erotic context, as does giving yourself over to me as your Master. You are still learning to trust me, not only with your mind, but with your body and your spirit."

His hand still on her shoulders, Liam dipped his head and kissed her lips. They parted eagerly, her tongue slipping out to meet his. Liam's cock, which had been hard from the moment he'd chained her to the wall for the water play, throbbed in his jeans. He had to fight the sudden impulse to throw her to the ground and take her then and there. Aware the conquest would be all the sweeter after he'd taken her on this new journey, he forced his body to behave.

Letting go of her shoulders, he stepped back. "It's time, sub Allie. Is your body ready to submit to me?"

Allie squared her shoulders. "Yes, Sir Liam. My body is ready to submit to you."

"Is your mind ready to submit to me, sub Allie?"

A look of resolve entered Allie's eyes. "Yes, Sir Liam. My mind is ready to submit to you."

"Is your spirit ready to submit to me, sub Allie?"

The softness returned, shoulders that had lifted letting go of their tension. "Yes, Sir Liam. My spirit is ready to submit to you."

Taking her elbow, Liam helped Allie step into the tub. He kept hold of her as she settled into a seated position in the warm water, her legs extended.

Crouching down on the thick rubber bath mat beside the tub, Liam extended his hand and tapped Allie's shoulder. Her eyes widened suddenly, fear blooming in her expression.

"You can do this," he urged. "I know you can. Lower yourself into the water. I will tap you when you may rise again." He waited a beat and then another, silently willing her not to fail, aware she would be angry with herself if she stopped things now.

After a moment, he saw her resolve return. She drew in a deep breath and leaned back, lowering the upper half of her body into the water and not stopping until it closed over her face.

Liam placed his hand over her nose and mouth, though the placement was largely symbolic, as she would hold her breath whether or not his hand was placed there. He could feel the tension in her body, and see it in the rigidity of her muscles. He looked up at the large wall clock, counting the seconds as the secondhand rotated around the face. At twenty seconds, he removed his hand and tapped her shoulder.

Allie sprang up like a character in a horror movie, gasping for air as she shook the water from her face. Liam struggled not to smile at her histrionics. "There, now," he said in a calm voice. "That wasn't so hard, was it? You did very well. Now we will do it again."

He tapped her shoulder again, and this time there was less hesitation before Allie lowered herself into the water. He counted to thirty before he gave her the signal to rise. Again she gasped and shook her head, though with less drama.

"Slow your breathing," Liam reminded her. "Take slow, deep breaths." He allowed her a few seconds and then tapped her shoulder once more.

Taking another large breath, Allie sank beneath the water.

Liam watched the clock, letting it move past twenty seconds, past thirty seconds, past forty seconds, all the while his hand over her nose and mouth. Allie began to twitch, pressing her face against his hand. "You can do it," he said loudly so the sound would reach her even beneath the water. "Just a little longer."

Though he could feel her rising panic, Liam held her another five seconds before tapping her shoulder.

Again Allie sprang up like a jack-in-the-box, her mouth wide open as she sucked in the life-giving air. "Oh, man!" she gasped. "That really scared me, Sir. I thought my lungs were going to burst."

"You're doing really well, sub Allie. I'm impressed for your first time. You're doing so well in fact, that I think we'll add another level to the exercise at this point."

Liam reached for the handle of the storage drawer at the base of the tub and pulled it open. He found what he was looking for and held it up for Allie to see. "This is a waterproof dual-action vibrator. I'm going to insert this in your cunt. Make sure it stays in place. You'll be under longer this time, and if you feel like you can't handle it, just focus on the pleasure. But remember"—he fixed her with a warning stare—"you are not to come. You do not have permission."

Allie's expressive face revealed both desire and trepidation as Liam applied lubricant to the both heads of the vibrator. "Stand up and spread your legs."

Allie obeyed, and Liam tried not to be too distracted by the water falling off her beautiful, bound body. His cock and balls ached as he slid the rubber penis into Allie's tight cunt and positioned the clit tickler in place. When he was done, he looked up at her. "Sit down in the water again. Make sure it doesn't fall out."

Allie sat carefully. Liam reached into the water and twisted the base of the vibrator, bringing it to life. He could hear its muffled whirr beneath the water.

Liam tapped her shoulder.

Drawing in a deep breath, Allie sank beneath the water.

His hand again covering her nose and mouth, Liam held Allie down for a full forty-five seconds. This time she didn't struggle or panic, though she did rear up as quickly as before when he gave her the signal.

Without giving her much time to recover, he tapped her shoulder, again keeping her down for forty-five seconds. When she burst out of the water, she cried breathlessly, "Sir Liam, that vibrator is really intense. I'm afraid I'm going to—"

"Control yourself," Liam interrupted. "You do not have permission."

He tapped her shoulder once more. As the second hand swept past the forty second mark and moved to fifty and then fifty-five, Allie began to push against his hand, panic making her body rigid, even as the vibrator brought her close to the edge of orgasm. Not until sixty seconds had passed did Liam remove his hand and tap Allie's shoulder.

She came up, gasping and sputtering, her chest heaving, her eyes wild. Sensing she was about to protest she couldn't take any more, Liam headed her off by saying, "The exercise is over. I'm pleased with you, my brave, courageous girl."

Allie visibly calmed at this, her mouth closing, her body relaxing. Liam reached into the water and turned off the vibrator, and then gently withdrew it from her body. "Let me help you up."

Liam stood and took Allie's elbow as she got to her feet. Working quickly, he had the rope unknotted and removed within a matter of seconds. Reaching for a fresh towel, he wrapped it around Allie's shoulders and helped her from the tub.

Not caring that she was still wet, Liam pulled her into his arms and held her close. He could feel her heart pounding against her chest and she was still breathing rapidly. Her soft, round breasts were mashed against his bare chest and his shaft was like a bar of steel between them.

He had intended to lead her to the recovery couch, but suddenly the iron self-control he'd been exerting since they'd entered the dungeon failed him. Clutching her, he sank to the thick rubber bath mat, pulling her down with him. He laid her on her back on the mat and scooted back to crouch between her legs, placing his hands on either slender thigh to hold her open for his kiss.

Hungrily, eagerly, he lowered his face to her damp sex and drew his tongue along the delicate, swollen folds. Allie shuddered, her fingers curling in his hair. He licked in a circle around the hard nubbin of her clit and then lapped along her inner labia as she panted and sighed. He suckled and teased her until her body began its telltale tremble. A low, feral moan issued from over his head.

Liam pulled away. He had her right where he wanted her. "No," he said forcefully. "You will not come. Not yet."

Allie lay as she was, knees bent, legs spread open in wanton invitation, her eyes closed, her head thrown back, the color high on her cheeks, throat and chest.

Liam ripped at his jeans, yanking them down and kicking them away as fast as he could. Lifting himself over her, he positioned the head of his cock at her entrance and nudged forward. It was as if tiny hands clutched at his shaft, pulling it inside as her vaginal muscles clamped down in a hot, tight welcome.

He lifted and lowered himself, swiveling his hips until his cock made contact with her sweet spot. Her strong legs wrapped around him, drawing him deeper inside. He focused on holding on, not wanting to come until he finished with his cock what he'd started with his mouth.

He didn't have long to wait, as it was only a matter of minutes before Allie began to tremble again, her hips bucking forward to meet his thrusts, her fingers digging into his back. "Oh god, oh god, oh god," she wailed, each word rising musically up a scale. "Oh god, oh, it's actually happening, this is real. Oh, oh, oh can I, can I…"

"Yes, sub Allie, yes, you can. And you may. Come for me, baby. Come for me."

While that first feigned orgasm in the leather sling had been very convincing, now that he knew Allie and her body, there was no mistaking that this was the real thing. She gripped him as if he was keeping her anchored to the earth, while her voice rose in a high-pitched keening wail. She thrashed against him, her cunt stroking him in its tight, sensual grip as a new gush of moisture lubricated their coupling.

Unable to hold back another second, Liam let himself come, thrusting hard with each climactic spasm until he collapsed, completely spent.

They lay that way for a long time, until their racing hearts eventually slowed, their breath returned to something approaching normal. Liam must have dozed for a moment, because he was roused by Allie's words.

"Wow," she said softly, the wonderment evident in her voice. "I can't believe you did that." And then, louder, "How did you do that? I can't come that way. I've never been able to come that way. What did you do? You're a miracle worker. You did it!" She laughed happily.

Liam lifted himself on his elbows and regarded her with an amused, tender smile. "No, sweetheart. *We* did it."

CHAPTER 9

Allie looked at her email account with dismay. She had twenty-two unread emails, most of them business-related. In the time she'd spent in Portland with Liam, she had been so caught up in their new love affair, she had barely glanced at her laptop, or given any thought to her jewelry business. The only texts she'd answered were those from Lauren, eagerly assuring her best friend that Liam was everything, and more, she'd hoped for.

She scrolled through the subject headers and opened an email from someone at her jewelry website who couldn't figure out how to use the shopping cart.

Allie went to the website to see if she could determine the person's issue. She quickly figured out the problem, which was a failure on their part to provide certain basic information necessary to complete the transaction. Reminding herself the customer was always right, Allie sent a quick, pleasant email apologizing for the inconvenience, explaining the issue, and giving the customer a fifty percent discount coupon for her troubles.

She read an exciting email from a jewelry boutique in San Francisco interested in carrying some of her necklaces, and then moved on to an email tagged as urgent from her part-time assistant, Marybeth, who was handling a few of the simpler aspects of the business during Allie's absence. Apparently, a very expensive shipment of Italian glass beads had arrived with most of the inventory smashed and broken, the result of poor packing, and the seller was giving Marybeth a hard time about a refund.

"Hey there, sexy. How's it going?"

Allie looked up from her laptop at the sound of Liam's voice. She had been working out on the veranda while he caught up on some work of his own inside. "Crazy, if you want to know the truth. I've been having such an amazing time with you this week that I guess I kind of forgot I actually have a business to run back in Boston. As much as I hate to say it, I think I have to go back home and take care of some things. I need to get back to my design studio and do some actual work, too, that is if I want to be able to pay my rent and fill all the new orders that are coming in."

Liam shook his head decisively. "Sorry, I don't think I can let you go. I might just have to leave you caged and bound in my dungeon, my sexual prisoner."

Allie laughed, though at the same time a shiver of delicious fear moved through her at the sexy fantasy. Then real life reasserted itself as she glanced at the still unopened emails before her. "I don't want to go, either, but I really don't have a choice. I've worked too hard to get where I am to let things fall apart."

She hesitated a moment as she did a quick mental calculation. "It would take me a few days to pack up more clothing, plus my jewelry inventory and some basic equipment. Then I could go back before month's end to sell my furniture and close down the apartment." Suddenly aware of the full implication of what she'd said, she added shyly, "If that's what we want, I mean. For me to move to Oregon permanently."

As she said it aloud, she realized it was definitely what *she* wanted. While she loved Boston, she had no family there, unless she counted Lauren as family, and there was really nothing else to keep her on the

East Coast.

To her vast relief, Liam smiled broadly. "Of *course* that's what we want," he confirmed. Then, with a frown, he added, "I understand you have to go back right now to take care of business. I was being selfish. It's just that I don't want to be apart from you, not for a week or a day or even an hour."

Allie didn't want to be apart from Liam, either. They had packed more into their week together than she had experienced in a lifetime. "Come with me for the trip," she blurted in sudden inspiration. "Then we don't have to be apart."

Liam's face clouded and he looked away. "I don't know," he said slowly. "I haven't really traveled since the accident. I'm not sure it's worth the hassle."

Allie opened her mouth to protest, but stopped herself as the experience at the Home Depot came back to her. While she had been angry over the episode with the little boy and the cart, she hadn't really considered on a gut level what it must be like to face the challenges Liam had to endure on a daily basis.

Gently, she said, "You won't be alone. I'll be with you, Liam. We can take our time. We can arrive extra early at the airport and we can be seated early so people don't jostle and annoy us." She stood and moved to him, placing her hand on his back. "I would love for you to meet my best friend, Lauren. And there are some pretty cool clubs we could check out while we're there, if we wanted to. It would mean a lot to me if you came back to Boston with me."

Liam seemed to weigh her words. Finally, he nodded. "You're right, Allie. I'm being foolish. Forgive me. I would love to come with you, as long as you promise to come back with me. To come home with me."

Warmth suffused Allie at the thought of making a home with this wonderful man, and she flung her arms around him. "I'll come back with you." Her voice caught with sudden emotion. "I'll come home with you. That's a promise."

In spite of a few glitches with seating and getting Liam's cane stowed overhead, the flight went smoothly, and they managed to navigate their way out of Logan and into an Uber cab without incident. The ancient elevator of her old, crumbling apartment building was broken, as usual. Allie became acutely aware of just how long and steep the climb up four flights of stairs was, with Liam, grim-faced and determined, limping beside her.

Finally at her door, Allie unlocked it quickly and pushed it open, gesturing for Liam to precede her. Once inside, they set down their bags. As Allie closed the door, all at once, Liam whirled around, letting his walking cane fall to the ground as he reached for her.

Placing his large hands on her shoulders, he pushed her gently but firmly against the door, leaned down and kissed her hard on the mouth. "I've been wanting to do that all day," he growled, when he finally let her go.

As Allie struggled to catch her breath, he reached for the buttons of her blouse, opening them one by one until it hung open. He pushed the blouse from her shoulders and reached behind her back, expertly unhooking her bra in one deft movement. Pulling the bra from her bare midriff, he leaned down to her, his lips closing over her rapidly stiffening nipple.

Allie couldn't stifle a moan as he licked and lightly bit first one nipple and then the other, while cupping her breasts in his hands. When he let her go, it was only to reach for the zipper on the side of her short skirt, which he tugged down. Slipping his fingers beneath the waist of her skirt, he pulled both it and her panties down her thighs until she stood naked before him.

Tugging at his jeans, he yanked them, along with his underwear, down to mid thigh. His cock sprang toward her like a divining rod, and Allie's cunt contracted with need and anticipation.

Reaching for her, Liam lifted Allie into his arms. Her legs automatically wrapped around his waist. He shifted her until their bodies connected, his hard shaft slipping easily into her wet heat.

They groaned in unison as Liam thrust deep inside her. A flash of pure, wanton pleasure heated her to a fever pitch. Through the haze of her lust, she saw Liam's head was thrown back, his eyes closed, a vein throbbing at the base of his neck in time with the pounding of his heart against her breastbone.

The whole situation was fiercely erotic, she stripped bare by her lover and slammed against the door, he too eager to wait another second before claiming her. How perfect, how romantic it would be if they could climax together. The problem was, she couldn't come in this position, she was sure of it.

You don't know that, a voice in her head retorted. *Everything is different now. You're with the man you love.*

The thought slipped into her mind without her permission. Allie had never, not once, been in love, not truly. Was it even possible to love someone after so short a time? Liam hadn't said the L word, and neither had she, yet here it was, shining like a beacon in her soul.

The man I love.

Liam's movements pulled Allie back into the moment. He was breathing hard, his body damp with perspiration as he stroked her with perfect friction. She loved the way he smelled. She loved the way he tasted. She loved the way he held her so she felt at once safe and more desired than she ever had been in her life.

His cock moved insistently inside her, his pubic bone rubbing just so against her throbbing clit. A buttery, melting warmth began to suffuse her entire body, moving from her toes up through her trunk, licking at her nipples, heating her neck and cheeks as if a flame had been ignited in her core.

"Oh god, oh god, oh god."

Allie heard the words, only processing a second later that it was she who had spoken. Realization arced through her like a bolt of lightning. As astonishing, as impossible as it was, she was about to come!

Permission. You need to ask permission.

Breathlessly, she cried, "Please, Sir, may I come? Oh. Oh, god."

Liam held her tighter as she trembled in her effort to hold off the inevitable until Sir Liam gave his permission. Just when she lost the last toehold of control, Sir Liam replied as breathlessly as she, "Yes, sub Allie. Yes, my love. Come for me. Come for your Master."

He pressed her hard against the door, holding her tight as he ejaculated inside her, his release accompanied by a low, sensual moan. Allie let herself ride the wave of their mutual pleasure, her body melting in the heat of an astonishing, powerful orgasm.

Finally, still holding her in his arms, Liam turned so his back was against the door and slid slowly to the ground. Still wrapped around him, Allie lowered her head to his shoulder and closed her eyes, deeply contented.

~*~

Liam hated to disturb Allie. She looked so peaceful: eyes closed in slumber, thick, dark lashes brushing her cheeks, lips softly parted. His leg was screaming, however, painfully cramped beneath her. As gently as he could, he lifted Allie and set her beside him on the carpet so she rested against the door.

Her eyelids fluttered open, and she smiled at him. "Oh, hey. Hi."

"Hi, you," Liam replied tenderly. He tried to keep the pain out of his face as he struggled upright. His jeans were tangled around his legs, and he pulled them, along with his underwear, up over his hips.

As Allie began to get to her feet beside him, he extended his hand to help her, grateful that she took it without appearing to be aware of his struggles. When she, too, reached for her clothing, Liam didn't stop her. In truth, he hadn't intended to make love to her the second they'd walked into her apartment. It had just happened, his desire suddenly overwhelming everything else.

But now, out of his element, his immediate need for her slaked, he decided not to assert his right to keep her naked. He was pleased when she pulled on her blouse without first putting on her bra. The fabric was sheer, and he could see the outline of her nipples poking alluringly against it. His cock nudged awake, and he gave it a silent order: *Down, boy*.

To distract himself, he looked around her small but nicely decorated apartment. She had partitioned the living room into three sections. Near the window was a sitting area with a loveseat and two chairs set around the coffee table. On the opposite wall she'd created an office space that contained a desk, over which hung a bulletin board filled with photographs and drawings that appeared to be jewelry ideas she must be working on.

Her work area, or design studio, as she'd called it, consisted of a large drafting table covered with clear plastic containers spilling over with glass beads, gold and silver chains, stones and polished gems, and bottles of what appeared to be various types of glue. There was soldering equipment and several trays of small tools, no doubt used in the creation of her art. In the far corner of the large room stood a small galley kitchen, and nearby a doorway that presumably led to the bedroom.

"This is really nice," Liam said. "You've definitely maximized the space."

Allie offered a rueful grin. "Thanks. I've done what I can with it."

"You've done a great job," Liam said sincerely. "It must be expensive living in Cambridge."

"You got that right," Allie said emphatically. "This tiny apartment costs me a fortune every month. Sometimes, it's been all I could do to make the rent. Forget about even considering buying a car or getting a bigger place. Every spare dime goes to expanding my business."

"Now there'll be more than dimes," Liam said with a grin. "No more exorbitant East Coast rent to pay."

"I'll pay my share of the mortgage, don't worry," Allie said quickly. "I always pay my own way."

Now it was Liam's turn to shrug. "Nothing to pay. I own that house free and clear. There is no mortgage. The settlement I got from the accident left me with enough money to live comfortably for the rest of my life. Like you, I work from home and am my own boss. The only thing I lack is someone to share my life with. The only thing I lack," he added, his voice softening, "is you. I love you, Allie Swift. I never want to let you go."

He held his breath as he waited for Allie's response.

"I love you, too, Liam. I've loved you all my life, even before I met you."

Her words blossomed in the very center of Liam's being, sparking their way up his spine and along every nerve. He moved closer and cupped her face, touching his forehead to hers. They stood that way for several long moments.

When they finally broke apart, they each took a breath and then laughed. "Listen to us," Allie said with a shake of her head. "We sound like a romance novel."

"No," Liam corrected. "They sound like us."

They laughed again, and then Allie said, "Where are my manners? You must be dying of thirst. I know I am. Airplanes always dehydrate me. Not to mention stand-up sex against the back of a door."

They moved toward the kitchen, which barely had space for the two of them. Allie opened the refrigerator and turned back to Liam. "I have Fresca, white wine and beer. If you're hungry, I have some wilted celery and a whole variety of condiments. What's your pleasure?"

Taking a pass on the celery, mustard, ketchup and even the capers, they both had the soda. Liam, who was thirstier than he thought, drank two full cans. The sweet drink made him realize he was hungry. "How about we order some takeout? Make an early night of it."

"That sounds like a plan," Allie agreed. "Do you like Middle Eastern food? There's an incredible Lebanese bistro just down the block that delivers."

"Works for me," Liam agreed. He would've been happy eating spaghetti out of a can, as long as he was with Allie. It occurred to him he was happier than he had ever been in his life, so happy he could almost forget the buried, jagged shard of guilt that never truly stopped ripping at the heart of him.

Almost, but not quite.

They fell into bed later that evening, but Liam wasn't ready to sleep. "I brought you a present," he said with a sly grin, showing Allie the rope he'd packed in his overnight bag.

"Ooooh," Allie said, her eyes widening with excitement. "Thank you, Sir."

"The pleasure is mine," he replied sincerely, his cock hardening.

He took his time securing her to the bed frame until she lay like a submissive goddess before him, spread-eagle in her ropes, naked and flushed, her hair wild on the pillow around her face. He clamped her nipples with alligator clips, turning the small knobs until her nipples were compressed and red, her chest rising and falling as she struggled to handle the erotic pain. He smacked her bare, smooth cunt with an open hand, making her cry out with each strike. At the same time, her clit rose hard beneath his palm, and the spicy sweet scent of her arousal filled his nostrils and fueled his lust.

When he finally released the clamps, he suckled away the pain. Once she had calmed, he straddled her chest and pressed the head of his cock against her lips. She opened her mouth as eagerly as a baby bird. He eased forward, sliding the full length of his shaft down her throat, aware in this position he was blocking her ability to breathe. He remained that way for several long seconds, until her eyes widened, her pupils dilating with a heady mixture of lust and fear that made his heart kick into high gear.

He pulled back slowly, allowing her to suck in a deep breath before plunging once more deep into her throat. "I own you, sub Allie," he growled, power moving through his veins like rocket fuel. Not yet ready to come, he repositioned himself between her bound, spread legs.

He lowered his face to her cunt, inhaling the perfume of her musk as he darted his tongue along her delicate, sweet folds. He brought her close to the edge of a trembling climax and then abruptly pulled away, replacing his tongue with the sharp crack of his palm against her wet, spread cunt.

Allie cried out in shock and pain. Excited, Liam smacked her again, and then again, until she began to twist in her bonds, whimpering softly. She said something he couldn't quite catch.

"What was that?" he asked, punctuating his words with another sharp slap against her hot cunt.

"Fuck me, Sir," she cried breathlessly. "Please fuck me, Sir Liam."

He wanted to resist her; to force her to beg, but he couldn't hold out another second. His balls aching, his cock throbbing, he lifted his body over her and thrust into her without warning or preamble, burying his cock to the hilt in the velvet clutch of her pussy.

He groaned at the sheer pleasure of claiming this beautiful, strong, lovely woman. Now that he'd said it once, it was easier to repeat, and Liam whispered into Allie's ear as he thrust inside her, "I love you, Allie. I love you."

"Can I..." she gasped, apparently unable to say more.

"Yes," Liam managed, just as a powerful climax rocketed through him.

He collapsed against her, their bodies slick with sweat, their limbs entangled, both too spent to move.

The car came hurtling out of nowhere, rushing toward him with the roar of its engine and the screech of its tires. He stared in frozen horror as the man behind the wheel smashed through the windshield, shards of splintering glass slicing the man's face into ribbons of blood as he landed with a terrifying thump onto Liam's car.

"You did this," the man cried, his eyes rolling with pain and rage. Liam swerved wildly on the road, trying desperately to regain control of his car. His feet had turned into lead, and he was unable to lift his foot, which pressed hard against the gas pedal as the car raced forward at an impossible speed.

The man remained glued to his windshield, as if held in place by suction cups. "You killed me," he cried accusingly. Liam could see his crushed skull through the ripped skin of what had been his forehead. Gobbets of gray matter were splattered, along with red splashes of blood, over the glass. Liam stared in horror as the man reached through the windshield, his mangled hand passing through the glass as easily as a ghost's. He gripped Liam's shoulder, shaking it hard as he moaned, "Your fault. Your fault. Your fault."

"Liam, Liam, wake up. You're dreaming. Please, wake up. It's only a dream."

Liam sprang up, his heart striking like a jackhammer in his chest. He reached for the steering wheel, desperately trying to control the car as it careened wildly over the road.

"Liam! Wake up!"

As Allie's words penetrated his sleep-soaked brain, Liam hovered for a moment between nightmare and reality, unable to make sense of where he was or what was happening.

"Liam," Allie said again, her voice cracking with emotion. "It's okay. You're okay. It was just a dream. You're here with me, safe in my bed." She brought her arms around him, and Liam realized he was shaking, his body bathed in sweat. "Safe in my arms," she added tenderly, pulling his head down to her breast.

All at once, Liam was overwhelmed by the lingering emotion caused by the nightmare. He struggled to push through the anguish as Allie cradled him in her arms. To his horror, he began to cry.

Allie stroked his head, making soothing sounds in her throat. "It's okay," she whispered gently. "It's okay to cry. I am your safe place, as you are mine."

Her words were like a sharp lance that pierced the poison-filled tumor of his guilt and grief, and his tears turned into ragged, ugly sobs. Allie continued to hold him and stroke him, gently rocking him as he wept.

Even in the midst of his tears, it occurred to Liam he hadn't cried at the actual time of the accident, or afterward when he had learned what had become of the other driver. He hadn't cried when Lila, her face a study in shock as she stared at him in the hospital room, his body plugged with tubes and needles, bloodied and bruised, had whispered that she couldn't stay.

Now he cried as if his heart would break, while Allie held him, and his heart, together.

~*~

Allie kept her arms around Liam for a long time after he had quieted. She held him until she was sure he was sleeping deeply, and, she hoped, dreamlessly. She understood that the car accident was the source of his nightmares, but she didn't understand the depth and the terrible grip in which they still seemed to keep him, even after a year's time.

Gently extricating herself from him, Allie turned over on her side, vowing she would learn the truth of his nightmares, hoping he would trust her enough to share what it was that still seemed to weigh so heavily on his soul.

When they woke the next morning, she waited for Liam to say something about the night before, but he did not. As they brushed their teeth, she could see his face was drawn and haggard. Gently, she asked, "How are you this morning? It was a rough night, huh?"

Liam's eyes slid away from the mirror, and he shrugged. "Sorry about that," he said brusquely. "I still have nightmares from time to time. It's no big deal."

"No big deal?" Allie began, but then she stopped, suddenly aware of how incredibly uncomfortable Liam had become. He held himself stiffly, as if steeling himself for a blow. She closed her mouth, uncertain how to proceed.

Maybe it just wasn't the right time. He had cried in her arms. It was hard for some men, for most men, to be so vulnerable in front of a woman. In spite of the intensity and the passion between them, the relationship was still so new. She would give it time. She would give him time to open up when he was ready.

Forcing brightness into her tone, she said, "Okay, then. We can talk about it later, whenever you're ready." The look of relief on his face was almost comical, if the subject weren't so serious, and Allie allowed herself a smile. "Before I get down to work, are you hungry? There's a fantastic Greek diner near here that makes fabulous corn muffins on the grill with tons of melted butter. I could run down and get some. Interested?"

Liam's lips lifted into a smile, even if the smile didn't quite reach his eyes. "Do they have coffee? Very strong coffee?"

"Pure jet fuel. And real cream."

"It's a deal."

CHAPTER 10

"Have you ever noticed women always go to the bathroom in pairs?" Martin Haller, Lauren's boyfriend, asked. They watched Allie's and Lauren's retreating backs as the two girls wove their way through the tables at the crowded restaurant—a trendy seafood place with a nice view of Boston Harbor. "What the heck is that about?"

Liam shrugged. "Men enjoy the play-by-play in sports. I think women enjoy the play-by-play on dates. They're probably dissecting us both right now, giving their opinions on how we're each doing so far. Important decisions are made in the ladies' restroom, I'm guessing."

Martin, somewhere in his late twenties, with dark, curly hair, intelligent brown eyes and a full beard, fingered one of the several gold hoop earrings he sported along his left ear as he grinned. "Hopefully we're both passing the secret girl-tests. Lauren talks about Allie all the time. She really misses her, but she's super glad the two of you have connected."

"I am, too," Liam said with a smile. "It's great they're such good friends, and both into the scene. My best friends back in Oregon are also into the scene. I don't have to leave out huge parts of my life and who I am when I'm around them, like I do with most vanilla folks, you know?"

Martin nodded. "I hear you, man. Even with all the BDSM-lite hype out there these days, most people don't really get the lifestyle, or approve of it if it goes beyond a little slap and tickle in the bedroom."

"Yeah," Liam agreed. "Not that we need or even particularly want their approval."

Martin lifted his beer mug toward Liam. "I like the way you think. Say, why don't you two come out with us tonight? We're going to The Hot Seat. It's a cool underground club—invitation only."

"Ah," Liam said, lifting his chin toward Martin. "That explains your duds." Martin wore a black knit top tucked into black leather pants, his feet encased in heavy, black combat boots.

Martin glanced down at himself and grinned. "Oh, this? Yeah, I guess, except I pretty much dress like this all the time during non-work hours. This is the real me, not the jacket and power tie shit I have to wear at the office."

"Well, it suits you," Liam said, glancing down at his own well-worn, faded jeans and wondering what it would be like to slip into tightly sculpted black leather pants. "I guess I go more for the rumpled look," he added with a self-deprecating grin.

"Hey," Martin shrugged. "Whatever works, right? So, what do you say, you guys up for the BDSM club? Hot Seat has all kinds of great equipment and toys. I'm pretty sure I can get you both in, if you're up for it."

"We have an early flight in the morning," Liam said slowly as he thought it over. Then he grinned, adding, "But, hey, sleep is for the meek, right?"

"Exactly," Martin agreed. "You gotta come. I have a new cane I can't wait to try out on Lauren's ass."

"Allie has something of an issue with canes," Liam replied. "An issue that I believe needs exploring."

Martin lifted his eyebrows. "Oh, yeah?" he said eagerly. "So let's explore. We could do a double scene. Maybe take turns on each of them. String 'em up side by side. Wouldn't that be a pretty picture?"

Liam considered this. It would indeed be a pretty picture—Allie with her tumble of unruly hair cascading down her long, slender back, suspended beside Lauren, a petite blonde with milky-white skin that probably showed a cane's welts to great effect.

He let the image go as he shook his head. "Not yet. I mean for Allie. She's not ready yet for a public scene with a cane."

They stopped talking as the girls approached the table and seated themselves. Lauren was a cute girl, with long, straight blond hair, large blue eyes, a button nose and a wide, sensual mouth. She turned to Allie with a grin. "Do you ever wonder what guys talk about when we go off to the bathroom?"

Allie looked expectantly at Liam, while Lauren regarded Martin.

Both men shrugged and, as if they had rehearsed it, said in unison, "Sports."

The girls exchanged an amused glance.

A waiter appeared with dessert menus. After they placed their orders, Lauren said to Martin, "I was telling Allie about the club tonight. Do you think we could get them in, too?"

Allie put her hand over Liam's, a tentative smile on her face. "What do you think, Liam? Would you like to check out a BDSM club here in Boston?"

"Sure," Liam said, smiling back at her as he turned his hand over and threaded his fingers with hers. "In fact, Martin was just telling me about the new cane he bought to use on Lauren's ass."

Allie's eyes widened, her hand fluttering to her mouth.

Apparently unaware of Allie's discomfiture, Lauren said eagerly, "It's gorgeous, Allie. You should see it. The handle is braided with burgundy leather, and there's this cool metal tip at the end of the cane that's sure to leave a wicked mark." She hugged herself and gave a theatrical shudder. "I can't *wait* to feel the burn."

Lauren's mobile features shifted from erotic longing to sudden excitement as she looked from Allie to Liam and back to Allie. "Hey, you guys could scene with us! Martin has lots of canes, right, Martin?" She glanced briefly at her boyfriend, but before he could respond, she rushed on. "And they have gear at the club, too. We could use one of theirs."

She placed her hand on Allie's arm and squeezed. "Wouldn't that be awesome, Allie? You and me in a double scene with these two gorgeous guys caning our asses?" She laughed happily. "We could compare welts afterward."

Allie looked anxious, her gaze flitting from Lauren to Liam and then back to Lauren. "Come on, Lauren," she said in a small, tight voice. "You know I don't do canes."

Lauren looked blank for a moment. Then she tossed back her long blond hair with a laugh. "What are you talking about, sweetie? You're with a *real* Master now. You do whatever *he* wants you to do." She held up a hand as Allie started to reply. "Yeah, I know, I know. You didn't *used* to do canes. I get that. You didn't used to do love, either, remember? That's all changed now. Right?"

Color splashed over Allie's cheeks, her shoulders lifting with sudden tension. She looked helplessly at Liam. "I don't—I mean, I'm not—that is…"

"It's okay, sub Allie," Liam said in a low murmur for her ears only. "I got this." Turning to Lauren, he said with a smile, "We'd love to come to the club with you guys. As to the rest of it"—he gave Allie's hand a gentle squeeze—"we'll play it by ear."

"Yes," Allie agreed with evident relief. Sassy humor returned to her tone as she added, "I'd love to watch Martin lay some wicked stripes on your butt, girlfriend. Better you than me!"

Martin, who had driven the four of them to the restaurant, stopped at Allie's apartment so she could change into something more suitable for the club. Liam, who had only packed jeans for the trip to Boston, waited in the car with Martin while the girls ran upstairs.

As they disappeared inside the apartment building, Martin twisted back to regard Liam. "So," he said, "you know, uh, Lauren told me about your car accident and stuff. Must have been pretty bad, huh? You get around pretty good with that cane, though, right?"

Heat tried to rise in Liam's face, but he refused to allow it. This was what he hated—the unwelcome attention of well-meaning but clueless friends and strangers. "Yeah," he said, trying not to snap, "it took some getting used to, but it's fine. I get around fine."

Martin nodded. "Awesome. I just ask because this club we're going to—it's literally underground. There are pretty steep stairs we have to go down to get in. I could call ahead. They have a bouncer there who I've personally watched carry a woman, wheelchair and all, down those stairs like it was nothing. Not that you'd need carrying," he added quickly. "But you know, if you needed assistance or whatever."

Aware Martin was just being thoughtful, Liam managed what he hoped was a gracious smile. "Not a problem," he replied. "I can handle stairs, but I appreciate your looking out for me."

They broke off their conversation about sports teams on the East versus the West Coast when the girls exited the building about fifteen minutes later. Lauren, Martin had informed Liam, had her club outfit hidden beneath the dress she'd worn to dinner. "Not that there's much to the outfit," he added with a sly grin.

Liam's cock jumped to attention and saluted at the sight of Allie as the girls approached the curb. Beneath an open cream-colored silk blouse she wore a black leather bustier that offered her round breasts up like lush, ripe peaches. Her skirt was short, the black leather stopping at mid-thigh to reveal long, lightly tanned legs. She walked with a sensual, sashaying sway on black high heels. All that was missing, he thought suddenly, was a collar. *His* collar.

Since he had met her, she had rarely worn much makeup, and needed none, but tonight she had applied a deep red lipstick to her sensual lips and some kind of glittery gold on her eyelids that brought out the copper and russet tones of her shiny hair.

As she slid into the backseat beside Liam, she placed her hand on his thigh. He had to press his lips together to keep from groaning with pure lust. "Jesus," he whispered, "you are fucking gorgeous." He was rewarded with a dazzling smile.

The Hot Seat entrance was located in the alley behind a BDSM clothing boutique, a doorbell beside its red metal door. Martin pressed the buzzer three times in rapid succession and then rapped twice against the door with his knuckles.

Allie leaned into Liam. "It's like a speakeasy in the twenties, right?"

"Yeah," Liam agreed. "Except instead of bathtub gin, we've got whips and chains."

Martin turned back with a grin and patted the large gear bag he'd slung over his shoulder. "Yep," he agreed with a laugh. "Right here."

"And canes," Lauren piped up. "Don't forget canes."

The lock clicked open noisily, and Martin pulled the door open. Liam gestured for the others to go first, and swung fairly easily down the narrow steps, avoiding the worst of the crumbling concrete as he maneuvered himself. *See, not so bad,* he told himself. *No big deal.*

Martin spoke quietly with the big, burly man who opened the door at the foot of the stairs. As the other three stood back, Lauren reached for the hem of her short dress and pulled it over her head without a trace of self-consciousness.

"You like?" she said to Allie and Liam as she executed a slow turn.

"What's not to like?" Allie quipped, echoing Liam's own thought. Lauren's ample breasts spilled over a red leather bra cut so low the top half of her areolas were visible. To complete the minimalist ensemble, she sported a matching red thong, the tiny triangle of leather leaving almost nothing to the imagination, set off sexily by sheer black thigh-high stockings and stiletto heels. The flesh on her ass and the backs of her thighs had the slightly mottled, ridged quality of someone who was whipped often and intensively, though it was clear the aftercare was good, the scarring minimal.

Liam let out a low, appreciative whistle, which earned him a saucy, satisfied grin from Allie's sexy friend. Perhaps inspired by Lauren's casual exhibitionism, Allie let the silk blouse she wore slip from her shoulders. Willowy and graceful where Lauren was round and voluptuous, Allie was, to Liam's taste, sheer perfection.

"You like?" she echoed, her smile suddenly shy as she, too, pirouetted for Liam.

"I *love*," he affirmed sincerely.

After a moment, Martin turned back and waved to them with a grin. "It's all good. Come on in." He then did a comical double take as he looked at the girls. "Oh, my, my, my. This is going to be *fun*. Give me that stuff," he added, gesturing toward the clothing they each held in their hands. "You won't be needing it for a while." He held out his hand and the girls both gave him their discarded garments, which he tucked into the gear bag.

The walls of the club had been painted black, the space lit by large sconces that resembled flickering candles. There were six separate scene stations set up around the perimeter of the large room, each one with different BDSM equipment, including a set of stocks, a medical bondage table, a spanking bench, a suspension web, and two St. Andrew's crosses.

There were perhaps twenty or twenty-five people milling about the small space. Racks of canes, whips and paddles had been strategically placed at each scene station, several of which were already occupied, scenes in progress as the two couples made their way through the club.

Along the back wall stood a shiny chrome bar with black and chrome swivel stools set in front of it. A tall, swarthy man with a heavy beard and multiple tattoos, clad in a black leather vest, stood behind the bar. "Evening, folks. Hey, Martin. Good to see you again. What can I get you and your friends?"

"Hey, Oscar," Martin said as they seated themselves at the bar. "Thanks. Just a couple of bottles of water, right, guys?" He looked to the other three, who nodded. As Oscar placed four cold bottles on the bar, Martin said, "You remember my sub girl, Lauren, and these are our friends Liam and Allie."

"Welcome to The Hot Seat," Oscar replied in a gravelly voice. His gaze shifted to the two women, his small, sharp eyes glittering. "Hopefully you'll be heating the seats of these two lovelies in short order."

"That's the plan," Martin said as he jumped down from his stool and scooped his bag from the floor. He placed two of the four unopened water bottles into the bag. "Thanks for the water, bro," he said to Oscar. He turned to the others. "Let's grab one of the crosses before it's taken." Reaching for Lauren's arm, he pulled her from the stool.

Lauren flashed an excited grin in Allie's direction. "Come on. I want you to watch."

At a nod from Liam, Allie dropped the other two bottles into her purse, and she and Liam followed the couple. As they walked, Allie leaned into him and slipped her arm around his waist. Something about the position made his walking cane nearly unnecessary, and he allowed himself to lean back against her, just a little.

At the cross station, Martin was already engaged in cuffing Lauren's wrists on either side of the X. He left her legs free. Liam and Allie came to a stop behind them. Liam could feel both Allie's excitement and agitation. He kept his arm firmly around her shoulders.

Several people joined them in a semi circle around the cross, the usual onlookers who provided a ready, eager audience for every scene. When Martin pulled the cane from his gear bag, he held it out for the onlookers to admire and then whipped it with an audible whoosh through the air. A small chorus of *oohs* and *aahs* erupted amidst laughter.

"Bring it on, man," one of the men called. "Mark her good."

Martin surveyed the group and raised his index finger to his lips to indicate quiet. To their credit, the group silenced at once. Martin turned his attention back to Lauren. Though she was in four-inch heels, Martin was a good foot taller than she. Leaning over her, he gripped a handful of her hair, which he coiled in his fingers, using it to pull her head back.

He kissed her roughly on the mouth, drawing an audible moan from her lips. The chemistry between them was palpable, like an electric force field that held them both in its thrall.

When Martin drew the metal tip of the cane down Lauren's spine, a shudder moved through Allie's frame, as if she were the one on the cross. Liam pulled his girl closer and kissed her hair.

Martin began to tap Lauren's plump, curvaceous ass in light, steady strokes that made the flesh jiggle pleasingly. Allie tensed again as the cane's stroke intensified, though Lauren remained the picture of calm serenity.

When the first stroke hit hard enough to leave a welt in its wake, Lauren's only reaction was a sigh. Martin moved to her side, his wrist flicking with expertise as he began to paint parallel horizontal welts over Lauren's ass cheeks. At the tail of each welt was a darker, deeper mark, the result of the metal tip.

Allie reached up for Liam's hand on her shoulder and gripped it hard.

Lauren had begun to breathe deeply, her shoulders rising and falling with each searing crack of the cane. She was, Liam saw, working with the pain, using her breath to ride each new wave. More people had gathered to watch the scene, everyone maintaining a respectful silence as Martin danced around his sub girl, wielding the cane with masterful precision. Lauren's bottom was striped with crimson welts, and Martin turned his focus to the expanse of flesh above the lace band of Lauren's stockings.

As the cane landed against the back of both thighs in unison, Lauren emitted her first real cry of pain. Martin struck her again, several times in rapid succession, leaving a series of welts in neat rows against the backs of her thighs. Her shoulders hunched, the muscles bunching with tension.

Lauren began to jerk at her restraints, and Liam saw the sheen of perspiration on her skin. Martin paused the caning a moment, moving to stand directly behind Lauren. He bent forward, whispering in her ear as he stroked her hair. As he spoke to her, Lauren visibly relaxed, her breathing slowing, her limbs loosening.

Liam pulled his eyes from the scene to regard his sub girl. She twitched nervously, her eyes wide with anxiety. Liam leaned close and spoke softly. "What is it, sub Allie? What's making you so skittish?"

"You don't know Lauren like I do," Allie replied in an anxious stage whisper. "She doesn't have boundaries. She never uses her safeword, no matter how far a guy might go. She'll never tell him to stop. What if Martin doesn't know that? What if he goes too far?"

"She's wearing his collar, sweetheart," Liam reminded Allie gently. "She trusts him. I trust him, too. Don't you? It's clear he knows what he's doing." He kissed the top of Allie's head. "I think maybe you're reacting off your own fear, rather than what's actually happening in front of you. I see a submissive woman accepting the caning her Master is lovingly giving her. She's where she wants to be. She asked that you witness this scene. I ask that you accept what you are seeing with grace and courage. One day soon it will be you there on the cross. One day, you will have enough faith and trust, not only in me, but in yourself, to get to where Lauren is now."

"It is time now, slave," Martin said, drawing them both back to the scene. His voice had taken on a deep, resonant tone as if he were speaking from a stage. "I am going to give you five wicked strokes. When I'm done, you will let go. You will soar."

"Yes, Master Martin," Lauren said throatily.

The crowd held its collective breath as the cane struck Lauren's ass, leaving a dark, vicious mark in its wake, a droplet of blood at the tail. "One," Martin intoned.

"Oh!" Allie cried. Liam pulled her close.

Martin struck again. "Two."

At the end of the fifth strike, Lauren's head fell slowly back. Instead of the twist of pain one might expect to see after such an intense caning, Lauren's lips were lightly parted, her eyes closed as if she were sleeping, her expression placid, even serene. She was utterly still. She didn't even appear to be breathing. She looked like an angel, floating in her own private heaven.

"Ooh," Allie sighed, holding the syllable for several long seconds, the awe evident in her tone.

"Wow," Liam agreed, equally awestruck. Somehow, Martin had sent his sub girl flying on command. It was something that had never even occurred to Liam to try. Yet there was no denying what he was witnessing. Lauren was in that powerful and secret place a good Dom could take his sub, but could never really follow. He could only stand back and watch, ready to catch and hold his charge when she finally drifted back to earth.

Martin dropped the cane and stepped directly behind Lauren once more. He extended his arms, covering Lauren's hands with his own as he rested his cheek lightly against the top of her head. Liam could feel the silent communion between them.

After several long moments, Martin stepped back. As if suddenly released from the same spell that had held Lauren, he moved quickly to open her cuffs. Turning back to Liam and Allie, he flashed a broad grin. "She's pretty fucking amazing, isn't she?" he asked with obvious pride.

"You got that right," Liam agreed sincerely.

"Amazing," Allie breathed. "Lauren? You back on planet Earth?"

Most of the onlookers had dispersed to find a more active scene. Lauren slowly turned her head. "Reluctantly," she said and then sighed happily. "I wonder if that's what heroin's like. If so, I totally get it." She gave a small laugh. "I'm glad submissive headspace doesn't kill you."

"Though it sure is addictive," Allie replied. Her answering laugh, however, sounded brittle to Liam's ears, and he turned to regard her more carefully. He could feel the tension in her body, and the edginess in her psyche. The caning had excited her, but it had also upset her, or perhaps more accurately, it had unbalanced her.

Martin, his arm around Lauren's shoulders, said, "I'm going to take my girl to the recovery room. I want to treat her welts so they don't scar."

The four of them moved to the back of the club, stepping through a doorway into a room that contained several deep sofas, reading chairs, and three padded massage tables. Martin and Liam helped Lauren onto a table where she lay on her stomach, her cheek resting against the soft, padded leather. Her face was suffused with a kind of shiny, sleeping joy, as if lit from the inside out.

As Martin applied salve to Lauren's welts, Allie crouched beside her. "Hey there," she said softly. "That was quite a caning you took. I don't think I could do that."

Lauren smiled sleepily. "You totally could, Allie. Canes are just one of those weird trigger things of yours. Hell, I've seen you take a single tail lashing that left you with marks the rest of the week. If you can handle that, you can definitely handle a cane. I promise."

Allie was quiet and Liam decided not to intervene. Lauren went on. "The cane is intense, sure. It stings like a bastard. But the pleasure you get from it, the masochistic high, is awesome. You're like that kid on the high dive, terrified to make the jump, even though you know you want to. But once you do it, Allie, trust me. You'll never want to come out of the water."

Allie glanced up at Liam. He could still see the anxiety in her expression, and feel the tension in her body. "Sub Allie, I think you need to refocus." He held out his hand and pulled Allie to her feet. "While Lauren recovers, I'm going to help you let go of some of this nonproductive stress you seem to be holding onto."

~*~

Liam led Allie back into the main club area. Though Allie had only been witness to the caning, she felt as if she had just endured a very intense scene herself, but without the satisfaction and closure Lauren had clearly enjoyed.

Several scenes were going on around them as they moved through the club, and more people had arrived to fill the space. Whips cracked, voices cried out in passion and pain, often followed by murmured awe, laughter and even applause. The air was redolent with sweat, musk and excitement.

Liam led her to a free spanking bench. Allie's ass tingled in anticipation. Yes, of course he'd known just what she needed, even when she herself did not.

She started to lie across the bench, but Liam stopped her. "Take off your skirt and panties," he said with calm, quiet authority.

Allie instinctively darted her eyes around the room to see who might be watching them. Then she recalled herself and focused solely on Sir Liam. "Yes, Sir." She reached behind for the zipper and drew it down her skirt. She dragged the skirt and her panties down her legs and stepped out of them. As she did this, Liam seated himself on the spanking bench and patted his lap.

Four men and two women had already gathered in front of them to watch whatever was going to unfold. Though Allie didn't especially mind being naked in front of strangers, she was glad to lie over Liam's lap, and moved quickly into position.

"Is she being punished?" one of the men asked, his hand not quite concealing the bulge at his crotch.

"She is being centered," Sir Liam replied.

"You have nice, big hands," one of the women said with a giggle.

"You can center me anytime, baby."

"I'll center you, you little slut," the man beside her said with a raucous laugh.

As at any BDSM club, there were always clueless people who didn't appreciate that a public scene was a gift, not a circus. As if reading her mind and sharing her disapproval, Liam leaned over and murmured in her ear, "Ignore them. Focus on me. Focus on letting go."

Allie turned her head so she faced away from the crowd. Liam stroked her bare ass, his other hand pressing gently on her lower back. He didn't warm her up, but instead began to strike her with a firm, rhythmic hand. Each hard blow sent a wave of erotic pain through muscle and bone, reaching into the core of her.

As her ass heated, the skin tingling and alive, the toxic tension inside her began to unwind. Each steadying blow freed her a little more, until every last drop of tension had eased into a peaceful flow.

Sir Liam continued to spank her with one hand, but the other hand had slipped its way between her thighs. She jolted at the sudden, unexpected whisper of his fingers moving over her clit and labia. At his touch, a fire ignited deep in her gut, and her clit began to throb, her cunt soaked with need. In a delicious dichotomy of pleasure and pain, he both spanked and stroked her.

It wasn't long before she began to shudder, the beginning of a climax mounting inside her in a rising wave. Even in the midst of the pleasure and pain, Allie marveled that she had spent a lifetime faking what now came so easily at the hands of this amazing man. It was no longer a matter of gearing herself up to make the right sounds and movements. Now it was a matter of holding on, of waiting until her Master gave her permission to let that wave crest into nearly unbearable pleasure.

She became aware of the sound of her own voice. "Oh god, oh god, oh god." Liam's palm and fingers moved in relentless tandem, drawing her ever closer to the edge of the abyss. She tried to form the words, to ask the permission necessary for release, but could only manage the first few words. "Please, may I..." before the chant reasserted itself. "Oh god, oh god, oh god..."

Thankfully, her merciful Master whispered in her ear as he continued to spank and tease her, "Yes, sub girl. You may."

The sting of his palm spiraled against the rapid patter of his fingers at her sex. With a groan, her body arched and spasmed, caught in a powerful, thundering orgasm that obliterated everything in its path.

As the roaring in her ears slowly abated, Allie became aware of laughter and applause. Startled, she turned her head toward the sound. For a moment, she had completely forgotten where she was, or that an audience was watching this intimate moment between Liam and herself.

She twisted back to look at Liam, who flashed a grin at her. "I think they approve," he said. "I know I do."

He flipped her effortlessly in his strong arms and gathered her close, kissing her eyelids, her nose, the corner of her mouth. "I love you," he whispered. "I may share the gift of your submission with others, but you belong to me. Don't ever forget that."

"No," Allie breathed happily as she snuggled against him. "I won't."

CHAPTER 11

Though the flight from Boston landed on time in Portland, just as they were taxiing to the gate, they were steered away from the terminal to wait on the tarmac for some unknown reason. After five minutes or so, the captain came on the intercom and mumbled nearly incoherently that, due to a construction accident outside one of the gates, they would be detained for ten or twenty minutes, or possibly more.

Allie, along with many of the passengers, groaned with frustration, but Liam just smiled. The aisle seat beside them was unoccupied. Allie sat in the window seat, Liam to her right. She was wearing a short skirt and Liam leaned over and said quietly, "Take off your panties and hand them to me."

Though Allie hadn't felt in the least sexy prior to this, his words sent her instantly to a submissive place. With a quick glance at the people directly across from them, all of whom were busy with their electronic devices, she lifted her hips and slid her panties down her legs. Bunching the bit of silk in her hand, she furtively passed it to her Dom.

Slipping it into the inner pocket of his sport jacket, Liam placed his left hand on Allie's right knee and began to inch it up her thigh. She swallowed hard, but knew better than to protest.

"Spread your legs," he ordered softly. "Give me access to what is mine." Allie obeyed, biting her lip as she thought about being observed, though at the same time, her nipples and cunt tingled, alert with expectation and desire.

To her relief, Liam reached for the blanket he had requested earlier in the flight and draped it over their laps. Returning his hand between her thighs, he pressed the heel of his palm against her vulva as he slipped two fingers inside her.

Allie pressed her lips together in an effort to stifle her moan.

Liam murmured into her ear, "I'm going to make you come. You don't have to ask permission. I don't particularly mind if you make noise, but you might want to keep it down."

"Easy for you to say," Allie tried to retort, but the last word ended in a gasp as he began to move his hand in a sensual, steady rhythm against her sex. Again she pressed her lips tight, breathing hard through her nose as Liam stroked her beneath the blanket.

It didn't take long for a climax to gather its spin inside her. She began to pant, perspiration dampening her forehead and throat. Liam moved his hand with expert and practiced ease as Allie squirmed and gasped beside him.

When he tipped her over the edge of a powerful orgasm, Allie couldn't stop the cry that escaped her lips. Liam's other hand clamped suddenly over her mouth, catching and sealing the sound as she spasmed against his perfect, relentless fingers.

When she had stilled, he removed first the hand from her mouth, and then the fingers buried in her cunt. He lifted his fingers to his nose and inhaled deeply, his face a study in bliss. Allie, blushing furiously, stole a glance at the passengers across the aisle, but, to her vast relief, no one was paying them the slightest bit of attention.

As if he'd timed it, the intercom clicked on once more, the captain announcing it was their turn to taxi to the gate. As some of the passengers applauded, Liam took Allie's face in his hands and kissed her lightly on the lips. "When we get home, sub Allie, we'll finish what we started here."

True to his word, the moment they entered the house, Liam dropped their bags, closed the front door and pushed Allie against it, just as he'd done when they'd arrived at her apartment back in Boston. Jerking at the fly of his jeans, at the same time he yanked up her skirt. Naked beneath, and still aroused and wet, Allie received his thick, hard cock eagerly, wrapping her legs around his waist as he took her, still standing, against the door.

As they slumped in a rumpled, post-coital heap to the ground, Liam turned and flashed Allie a grin. "Welcome home, my sweet girl."

As the weeks edged into a month since their return from Boston, Liam and Allie settled into an easy, sexy and satisfying routine. Allie sometimes lost herself in her jewelry making for hours on end, forgetting to eat or even pee until her body protested enough to get her attention.

During these times, Liam usually left her undisturbed, except to bring her something to eat or massage her shoulders for a few minutes. Sometimes, especially when she'd been working a while, he would describe what he planned to do to her in the dungeon once she was finished with whatever she was doing.

As was probably his intention, when he did that, Allie generally lost all interest in the project at hand. Within minutes of his sexy promise, she would present herself naked and on her knees, her arms raised, fingers laced behind her neck. She would say what had become her ritual greeting at that time. "I am ready and eager to serve you, Sir Liam."

If Liam were working on his computer, sometimes he would

respond only with a nod, leaving her to wait quietly on her knees for her Master's attention. The old Allie would have fidgeted impatiently, but now she possessed a new, serene patience that left her happy to wait for Sir Liam to turn his masterful gaze her way.

Other times he would close the lid of his laptop promptly and stand to face her. She loved it when he lowered his jeans and underwear and pointed to his cock. She would scoot eagerly to kneel between his legs and worship his beautiful shaft and balls. Sometimes he would let her continue to completion, gripping handfuls of her hair as he ejaculated deep in her throat.

Most times, however, he would stop her before she took him too far. He would lead her down to the dungeon instead, and take his time with slow, sensual and erotic torture, sometimes with a flogger or paddle, with clips, cuffs, clamps and rope but, so far, never with the cane.

"You will have to ask me for the cane, sub Allie," he'd told her one day when she'd mentioned with both fearful hesitation and desire that he had yet to introduce her to its dark pleasures.

That had been the week before, and she'd become increasingly obsessed with the idea of a full-blown caning session. Memories of the intense scene between Martin and Lauren at the club dipped and swooped at the window of her mind like a flock of trapped, persistent birds.

Finally, curiosity and desire won out over fear. That morning just after breakfast, Allie had presented herself before Sir Liam and asked in a tremulous voice, "Please, Sir. Will you cane me today?"

Now Allie stood on a thick rubber pad in front of a full-length mirror in their dungeon. Chains hung from a low beam over her head, wrist cuffs waiting to receive her. She could see Sir Liam behind her, a long, thin rattan cane in his hands.

"It's strange, isn't it?" He was watching her, his eyes sparkling with focused intensity. "That something so simple, almost delicate, can deliver such a powerful experience?" He ran his fingers sensually over the rod, his tongue gliding over his full lower lip.

"Yes, Sir," Allie whispered. In spite of her desire, in spite of the fact she had asked for this, a small knot of fear had formed just behind her breastbone.

"Here." He moved to Allie's side and held out the cane. "Examine the cane that I'm going to use on you today."

Allie took the offered cane. The black suede curved handgrip resembled an umbrella's handle. The cane was about two feet long, the rattan smooth and polished beneath her fingers. A jolt of nervous excitement shot through her heart en route to her cunt.

She looked over at the rack that held various floggers and whips. They were made of soft, sensual leather, despite the erotic pain they were designed to cause. But this cane in her hands seemed designed purely to inflict pain. She flashed to an image of Lauren, her ass and the backs of her thighs welted with dark, angry lines that would leave bruises and marks for days to come. She shuddered at the memory, fear nearly outweighing masochistic lust.

"Tell me what you're thinking."

"I'm afraid," Allie replied honestly. "I want it, but I'm afraid."

"Because?"

Allie pondered this. It wasn't pain per se she feared. Indeed, she welcomed erotic pain, aware of where it could take her. It was the cane itself. Something about it she didn't quite understand. "I don't know," she answered.

"I think you're frightened because you're focusing on the potential damage a cane can do. And yeah, in the wrong hands, it can do some pretty severe damage. But then"—he shrugged—"anything can do damage in the wrong hands. It's about intent, knowledge of the instrument and paying attention to your body and your reactions."

He moved closer and stroked Allie's hair. "Remember, I'm experienced with a cane, and while I plan to mark you, you know I would never harm you. I won't give you more than you can handle. And I should remind you, sweet sub girl"—his mouth quirked at the corner—"you can handle far more than you think. You've proved that over and over."

Allie smiled at this empowering remark, some of her anxiety ebbing away. "Yes, Sir," she said. "Thank you, Sir."

"Now," Sir Liam said, "you will kiss the cane and we will begin."

Allie touched her lips to the side of the cane and then handed it back to her Master.

He moved to stand just behind her, turning her so they were both facing the mirror. Regarding her image, he said, "For this session I'm only going to secure your left wrist. You'll need your right hand free. We'll use this spreader bar to keep you still." He pointed to the three-foot metal spreader bar, ankle cuffs attached on either end. "I will cane you until it pleases me to stop. You may speak at any time. Feel free to cry out as you need to.

"While I cane you, you will rub your pussy, not as a distraction, but as an enhancement to the pain. I want you to experience the sensations together. Ultimately, for you, they will become one and the same. As we progress with cane training, you will learn to associate the sting of the cane with the throb of your clit. As flogging and bondage are for you now, so, too, caning will eventually become as sexually stimulating to you as my tongue or my cock."

Allie tried to keep the skepticism from her expression, but apparently failed, because Sir Liam laughed and shook his head.

"It's okay," he said, his eyes crinkling with merriment, though it didn't hide the glitter of raw lust just beneath. "You don't have to believe me. Right now all you have to do is obey."

Sir Liam raised Allie's arm to the dangling restraint. She watched in the mirror as he closed the leather cuff over her wrist, securing her arm high over her head. Next, he crouched in front of her, tapping her legs to indicate their position so he could lock her ankles into the cuffs at either end of the spreader bar.

Rising, Sir Liam stepped behind Allie, cane in hand. Allie regarded herself in the mirror. Faint marks lingered on her breasts from the single tail lashing he'd given her the night before. Her already swollen labia pooched between her spread legs. While the cane frightened her, she couldn't deny how turned on she was.

She focused on the man behind her. Shirtless, he wore the black leather pants and black boots she had bought for him at her favorite BDSM clothing boutique in Boston their last day there. He was the very picture of masculine dominance, and she could have stared at him all day.

He met her gaze in the mirror, his eyes smoldering. "Lick your fingers," he ordered, "and then I want you to rub your cunt. I'll let you know when you can come."

A thrill of delicious, erotic fear rippled through Allie's frame. Yes, she was afraid, but at the same time she wanted this. More than that, she *needed* it. She licked her fingers and placed them against her aching sex.

"Yes, Sir Liam," she said breathlessly, her nipples tingling.

Sir Liam whipped the cane several times in the air. In spite of her arousal, Allie's gut clenched reflexively at the sound.

"I'm going to start lightly," he informed her. "Your job is to continue to stroke yourself, no matter what I do or how much it hurts. I'm going to mark you. Together we'll move past any lingering fear you've wrapped around the idea of caning. I'm literally going to whip it away."

He gave her a few moments to absorb his words, his beautiful green eyes boring into hers in the mirror. "Are you ready, sub Allie? Do you still wish to submit to the sting of my cane?"

"Yes, Sir Liam," Allie replied resolutely. "I want this. I need this."

Sir Liam nodded. "You do need this. I'm honored to be the one to give this gift to you."

He began to tap lightly against her ass with the side of the cane, striking both cheeks at once. The pleasurable sensation warmed her flesh as the blood increased its circulation beneath the skin. "Keep your hand moving," Sir Liam reminded her. Allie, distracted by the caning, resumed the swirl of her fingers against her sex.

Slowly but surely, Sir Liam increased the intensity of his stroke. Pain began to edge its way over the pleasure, but it was nothing Allie couldn't handle, hadn't handled many times before.

Then came the first searing stroke. Unlike the small, quick burn of a single tail, or the all-encompassing thud of a flogger, a long, thin brand of pain seared across both butt cheeks.

"Ow!" Allie cried, her entire body tensing at the blow.

"Embrace it," Sir Liam said. He struck her again, even harder.

Allie squealed, twisting reflexively away from the cane's arc.

"Sub Allie," Sir Liam said, his voice firm. "You are out of position. Stand still and put your hand back where it belongs. Rub your cunt while I cane your ass."

Allie forced her trembling fingers to relax as she touched her swollen, moist sex. Fear and lust tumbled together inside her, dragging her along in their undertow.

He struck her a third time and then a fourth time, once on each cheek. The blows were quick and sharp, the pain edging into something hot, dark and sensual deep in Allie's core.

Allie absorbed the pain, her breath sharp in her throat.

"This one will be harder, sub Allie. You will accept it with grace."

He met her eye in the mirror once more. She swallowed hard but managed a small nod.

The stroke was like a knife cutting through her flesh. Allie cried out, tears leaping into her eyes. Her heart was hammering in her chest and pulsing in her throat. Her lungs felt as though they had collapsed, and she couldn't seem to catch her breath.

Sir Liam took a step back and tilted his head as he regarded Allie's ass. "Whoa," he breathed. "You should see these awesome marks. You'll be so proud of yourself, sub girl."

There was fire in his eyes as he met her gaze in the mirror, but his expression gentled as he regarded her. Lowering the cane, he placed a hand on her shoulder and gave it a gentle squeeze. "Breathe," he reminded her. "You're doing so well. I'm so proud of you, sub Allie. I want to take you a little further, okay? I know you can do it. Embrace the pain and the fear. Harness it and let it empower you."

Allie nodded, her lungs filling and easing as she drew in and then released a deep, cleansing breath. She looked at herself in the mirror. A rosy flush had bloomed over her chest, throat and cheeks. Sir Liam, behind her, moved his hand from her shoulder to the back of her neck, his grip gentle but centering.

"Are you ready to continue?" he asked.

"Yes, Sir," Allie said, surprised at the firmness of her tone. "Please, Sir."

Dropping his hand from her neck, Sir Liam stepped back and lifted the cane. Allie slid a finger into the tight, wet heat of her cunt. As the cane sliced against her ass, the fire of its stroke caused her vaginal muscles to clamp down on her finger. She gasped, but didn't cry out.

When the cane hit again, she began to rub her fingers against her swollen clit. Pleasure and pain wound around her psyche with the silken strength of a spider's web.

The cane struck again, a line of pure fire where her ass and thigh met and, for the moment, stark pain obliterated everything in its wake. But then, just as quickly, it metamorphosed into pure, raw desire.

"Fuck," Allie moaned, the word more an affirmation than a protest.

Again and again the cane whipped against her flesh as her fingers flew between her legs. Tears welled in her eyes, spilling down her cheeks. Pleasure tugged at her senses, the rise of an impending climax gripping her loins. She heard a deep, lowing sound and realized dimly it was her own voice groaning in time to the relentless stroke of the cane.

"Fuck. Fuck, fuck, fuck." The word ejaculated from her lips with each sting of the cane. Her fingers moved in time to its pulsing caress. The fire licking over her ass like flames began to melt and meld into the heat generated beneath her fingers.

Her eyes fluttered shut, her head falling back of its own accord, her lips parting. The cane whistled and struck, the fire flicking directly through her sex, as if her fingers and the cane were somehow one and the same. Allie felt light, as if her body had lost its mass, its gravity. If she hadn't been tethered, she might have floated into the air, levitated by the combined, frenzied dance of the cane and her fingers.

"Yes," Sir Liam breathed from somewhere far away. "Yes, yes, yes.

You're nearly there."

She might've been climaxing, her body spasming in paroxysms of pleasure. It was possible she was crying, or laughing. Maybe both. Whatever was happening, it was like nothing she had ever experienced. Pain as a descriptor did not capture the fierce intensity. Pleasure was far too weak a word. The combined experience lifted her, propelling her out of herself, out of time. And then a rolling wave of pure, blinding sensation covered her senses, blotting out the world.

Allie opened her eyes, completely disoriented. She was on her knees, facing the mirror, leaning heavily against Liam, who sat just behind her on the mat, his legs on either side of her. As they made eye contact, he smiled with evident relief. "There you are. You left the planet for a minute or so. Are you okay?"

Allie thought about this as she regarded her image in the mirror. Her face was tear-streaked and flushed, her hair tousled, her nipples red and erect. As she came more fully to herself, she became aware not only of the stinging skin of her ass and thighs, but of the sense of deep, profound well-being that suffused her.

A smile moved over her face, lighting her eyes. "More than okay."

"You did even better than I expected," Liam said with an answering smile. "I would say you've conquered your fear of the cane. You're pretty amazing, Allie."

Allie nodded emphatically, her smile segueing into a broad, proud grin. "Oh, yeah. I'm, like, totally awesome!" They both laughed.

"You want to see the marks? They're gorgeous."

"Oh!" Allie jumped up excitedly and turned away from the mirror, twisting back to see. "Ooh," she said again, this time lingering on the vowel as she stared in awe at her ravaged ass.

He had painted dark red welts in even, parallel lines across both ass cheeks, several more marking the backs of her thighs. A few of them were raised, the ridges of abraded skin like badges of submissive courage over her flesh. There was no question—this was the most intense whipping she had ever received. She stared at the welts with horrified fascination that quickly segued into a quiet, fierce pride. She had endured a full-fledged caning. More than that, she had welcomed it.

She reached back a tentative hand and lightly touched one of the welts.

Liam, watching her, said, "I have a special salve I save for really intensive marking. A pharmacist friend of mine in the scene compounded it for me. It's a combination of Arnica and a powerful antibiotic cream, along with some healing herbs. Your marks will last a few days, but there will be no scarring."

Allie whipped around to face her lover. "I'm so happy!" she cried. She threw her arms around Liam's neck. He brought his arms around her waist as he dipped his head to hers. Their lips met for a long, lingering kiss.

When they finally parted, Allie added softly, "Thank you, Sir Liam, for taking me where I needed to go."

"Thank you, sub Allie, for letting me."

Though Allie missed Lauren, she really didn't miss much else about Boston since she'd left for good the month before. Happily, Martin and Lauren were planning a visit in the near future, as soon as they could coordinate their vacation time. Meanwhile, Matt and Bonnie had had Allie and Liam over for dinner a couple of times, and Liam and Allie had reciprocated. Allie quite enjoyed being part of a couple—not only for the sexual and BDSM intimacy, but for the vanilla fun of entertaining and enjoying friends.

Bonnie had shared with Allie that, since she'd entered the picture, Liam was like a new man. She hadn't really understood the extent of his reclusiveness following the accident. From what she could discern, he had basically shut himself off from the world.

But he was back, happy to socialize, willing to meet new people, and fully engaged in their relationship. Matt and Bonnie had invited the two of them to their favorite BDSM club, Paradise Found, to celebrate Liam's birthday that Saturday night, now only two days away. Liam, though he'd seemed to hesitate at first, had agreed they should go. Allie was very excited at the prospect of going to the club with Matt and Bonnie, both of whom had expressed strong interest in a shared scene.

Allie had been working off and on in secret on his present for the last week, ever since the parts she'd needed for it had arrived at Bonnie's house. She kept the project hidden beneath her worktable, lost in a jumble of supplies Liam would never think or want to go through.

A new idea for the filigreed top piece came to her suddenly in the middle of the night, waking her from sleep. Allie glanced at the clock beside the bed. Though it was still dark out, she was surprised to see it was already nearly five in the morning. She wouldn't get back to sleep until she brought the idea to life, so she slipped quietly out of bed and padded silently out of the bedroom.

She was soldering a delicate piece into place when she heard Liam's voice from their bedroom. She pricked her ears, her heart quickening.

Another nightmare.

Once every few weeks, he woke in a sweat, his eyes wild, his breathing ragged. Each time, she'd soothed him back to sleep, but every episode left her worried and sad. She had talked to Bonnie about it, wondering aloud if it was normal that he still had these nightmares a year after the accident.

"The other driver died," Bonnie reminded her. "He was the father of three children. Liam did go to therapy for a few sessions when it happened, but from what you're telling me, clearly there are still demons doing damage inside his head."

Allie had tried a time or two to broach the subject, gently suggesting he might want to return to therapy, but so far, while Liam seemed to listen and ponder her suggestion, he hadn't taken any action.

Allie quickly put away her project beneath her worktable and hurried across the hall to the bedroom to comfort her lover.

"No, no, no," he moaned, urgency in his tone. Allie could see from the light in the hallway that he was thrashing, caught in the throes of his nightmare.

She touched his shoulder lightly. "Liam. Liam, honey. Wake up. Wake up, it's okay."

"Stop it, you idiot!" he cried. "Put the phone down! Put the fucking phone down!"

What the hell? That was new.

Allie shook his shoulder more insistently. "Liam. Wake up."

His eyes flew open as he shot upright, his entire body rigid. "What?" He cried. "What is it? Who? What?"

"Shh," Allie said soothingly, though her heart clutched with sympathetic anxiety. "You're awake now. It was the nightmare. You were talking in your sleep."

She took the bottle of water from beside his bed, unscrewed the cap and handed it to him. As he drank, she ventured, "You said something different this time. Something about a phone."

Liam's eyes met hers and then skittered rapidly away. "I did?" he said, his head averted.

"Yes. You said, let me see…" Allie regarded the ceiling a moment as she tried to recall his exact words. "You said, 'Stop it, you idiot. Put the phone down. Put the fucking phone down.'"

"Oh, my god," Liam breathed. "Oh, my god." He looked at her, his face stricken. To her shock, tears formed in his eyes and rolled down his cheeks.

Alarmed, Allie squeezed his arm. "What is it, Liam? What does it mean? Why are you crying?"

Liam looked surprised and then confused. Slowly he lifted his hand to his cheek and then regarded his finger, which was wet with his tears. "I don't know."

Something in his tone sounded false. "Liam?" He didn't look up. "Liam," Allie said again, a little more forcefully. "What is it? What's going on?"

"Oh, Allie," he said, the pain in his voice driving a knife of pity and compassion through her heart. "If you knew…" He dropped his head into his hands.

Allie scooted closer and placed her hand on his shoulder. "What is it? Talk to me."

Liam was silent for a long moment, his face still hidden in his hands. Finally he whispered, "I've never told anyone. No one knows."

A deep sense of unease clutched at Allie's innards, but she forced herself to remain calm. She would handle whatever it was. They would handle it together. "You can tell me, Liam. I'm here for you. I'm your safe place as you are mine, remember?"

Slowly, he lifted his head, his face a mask of anguish. "You're right,

Allie. I owe you the truth. You trusted me with your secrets. It's time I do the same."

Allie waited, silently sending him all the strength and love she could.

"It's my fault, Allie," Liam finally said. "That guy is dead because of me. Those kids have no dad because of me."

Allie stared at him in confusion. "What? The guy was drunk and his car jumped the median. How could that possibly be your fault?"

Again he paused, this time for so long she thought he wasn't going to answer.

"Liam?"

He took a deep breath, as if girding himself, and then, speaking so softly she had to strain to hear him, said, "I was texting. I was texting on my stupid phone when the accident happened." He looked away, his words tumbling together in a rush, he went on, "I know it's totally stupid, but Lila"—he cut himself off with a press of his lips, but then made himself continue—"Lila and I had been having one of our endless arguments. I was using my thumbs instead of Siri, so my eyes weren't on the road. I glanced up and saw that car heading toward me at a million miles an hour."

Finally he looked at Allie, his expression at once tragic and beseeching. "Don't you see? If I hadn't been texting"—his voice cracked and he cleared his throat—"maybe I could have swerved away in time. Maybe that guy would still be alive." His voice cracked again, and he swallowed hard, wiping angrily at his eyes.

"Oh, Liam, no," Allie burst out. "No, that's all wrong. How long were your eyes off the road—two seconds? Three?" When Liam didn't respond, she went on earnestly, "There's no *way* that accident could have been prevented, even if your eyes had been glued to the road."

"You don't know that," Liam countered miserably.

Allie glanced out the window as she pondered this, an idea popping into her head. The sky was lightening outside, color edging over the windowsill. She didn't voice her idea, instead saying gently, "It's time you let yourself heal. It's time to forgive yourself, no matter what your role might have been."

"I know," Liam said quietly. "Maybe I'll do what you and Bonnie suggest and go back to that therapist. I don't like to think my shit is affecting someone else—affecting you."

Allie nodded. "I love you," she said simply, her heart warming at his answering smile.

"Me, too, you," he replied. "More than anything in this world."

Relieved the nightmare seemed to have fully released him from its dark hold, Allie asked, "Do you think you can go back to sleep?"

Liam shook his head. "No way. I'm totally awake. How about you?"

"Same here," Allie agreed, not mentioning she had already been awake and working on his secret gift. "How about I get some coffee going while you wash up?"

"Excellent idea." Liam swung his legs over the side of the bed. As he moved, he turned his face, but not before she saw the spasm of pain that twisted it into a grimace. That accident, she thought grimly, would be with them forever.

While Liam showered and shaved, Allie put on the coffee, slid some frozen biscuits into the oven, and hurried into his study. She hesitated a moment, worried about violating his privacy, but decided her goal superseded the moral dilemma.

Moving with purpose, she went to the filing cabinet in the corner of the room and pulled open the top drawer. There were many files, each one with a neatly labeled tab containing the name of an individual or a company. Work files, she could see.

The second drawer contained home and car insurance files, receipts and various other personal documents, nothing that pointed to the financial settlement or other details of the accident.

In the bottom drawer, she found what she was looking for, though her task, she saw, wasn't going to be easy. Unlike the other neatly organized drawers, this one was crammed with dozens of manila folders filled with mountains of paper. Many of the folders weren't labeled at all, and for a moment, she despaired of finding what she sought without spending an inordinate amount of time.

Crouching in front of the open drawer, she fingered rapidly through the mess, breathing a sigh of relief when she found the file she was seeking, labeled in the same strong, neat hand as those in the upper drawers: *Police Report.*

Pulling the file from the drawer, she flicked it open and quickly scanned the report, looking for basic data she hoped would mitigate Liam's concerns over his culpability. The first few paragraphs noted the condition of the cars, the injuries and the fatality sustained as a result of the collision, and the surviving driver's condition at the scene. Liam, the police noted, had been wearing his seatbelt. Witnesses at the scene stated he had been driving in the proper lane at a safe speed. There were diagrams on a pre-printed map, the cars placed on the grid to show their positions at the time of the accident. The notes on the map indicated Liam had swerved to the right just before the vehicles collided, shifting the point of impact from head-on to the front left and side of his vehicle.

Allie flipped to the last page of the report, an addendum dated a week after the initial report.

After regaining consciousness shortly after admission to Providence Portland Medical Center, Mr. Byrne signed consent to release information to the police regarding his mental status while driving, as well as cell phone usage.

The blood test performed during admission at the hospital revealed no alcohol or drugs in his system.

As Allie read the next section, her mouth fell open, and she lost her balance, falling back from her crouch onto her butt on the carpet. *Upon examination, the investigator determined there had been no incoming or outgoing phone calls or texts received during the minutes leading up to the accident.*

Allie startled at the sound of Liam's voice. Looking up, she saw him standing in the doorway.

"There you are," he said with a smile. "I heard the oven timer going off so I—" He broke off, his smile falling away, his eyebrows furrowing. "What're you doing, Allie? Why is the filing cabinet open? Why are you going through my things?"

"Evidence," she said, aware he might be angry at the breach of his privacy. There was too much at stake to worry about that right now. "I wanted to find something, anything, to help us really understand what happened that day." Allie rose to her feet. "Have you ever read the police report, Liam?" She waved it toward him.

Liam scowled and turned away. "I didn't need to read it," he said, both anger and defeat in his tone. "I lived it."

Allie moved quickly toward him. Gently, she touched his arm. "You need to read it now." She held the pages in front of him and pointed. "Right there. Read what it says, Liam. Please."

CHAPTER 12

Liam sat at the kitchen table, the police report before him. "This is so weird. I can't make sense of it." He stared down at words that flew in the face of what he knew to be true. He didn't remember the police being in the emergency room. He didn't recall signing any kind of consent, though apparently he must have done so. He looked up at Allie. "The pieces don't fit together."

Allie set a mug of coffee on the table by Liam's elbow. "We'll figure this out together. It's a mystery right now, but it's a good mystery."

Liam looked up at her, desperately wanting to believe her, though his heart told him something different. He reached automatically for the coffee and took a sip.

The entire reality of his life for the past year had been suddenly flipped on its head. It said right there in black and white that he hadn't been texting in the seconds leading up to the accident. And yet, he *had* been. Did the investigator deliberately cover up Liam's culpability for some reason? Or maybe the phone had been damaged during the collision, somehow erasing whatever data had been stored? Liam's head throbbed with the effort of sorting through the confusion.

Allie set a plate of biscuits on the table, along with butter and blackberry jam. She cut open a biscuit, spread butter over each side and spooned on some jam. She put the prepared biscuit on a plate and pushed it toward him.

"Thanks." In spite of his turmoil, Liam appreciated her sweet domesticity.

As she prepared a second biscuit for herself, Allie said, "So, tell me again. You say you remember texting with Lila in the moments before the crash, right?"

"Yeah. We were having an argument about something stupid." He smiled ruefully. "We were always having arguments, seems like. I don't even remember what it was about. Oh, wait." He squinted at the middle distance, the memory of their texted conversation suddenly tumbling back into his mind with vivid clarity.

"I remember now," he said. "It was about the wedding ceremony. She wanted to wear a heavy chain slave collar with her bridal gown and carry a leather flogger down the aisle instead of a bouquet. She was adamant about it."

Even as he said the strange words, he realized how completely ridiculous they sounded. Not only ridiculous, but incongruous with the preparations Lila had made for the wedding. She had invited friends and family who knew nothing about their lifestyle, both sets of parents included. She had spent a fortune on a designer wedding gown, and there was no way in hell she would have wanted to wear chains in lieu of her grandmother's pearls.

"Are you serious? She really wanted to do that?" Allie asked, echoing his thoughts.

Liam shook his head, as if he could somehow shake everything back into place. "I don't know," he said slowly. "It does sound pretty crazy, now that I'm saying it out loud. But I have this distinct memory." He paused, thinking it over. "It's really weird, though, because I never text when I drive."

He frowned, recalling the scenario—the phone beeping on his lap, looking down to see her message. Which was also odd, since he never kept his phone on his lap, where it might slip down between his feet if he had to stop suddenly.

"Something isn't right here, Liam," Allie said, interrupting his thought process. "The pieces aren't fitting together. The police report says definitively that you weren't using your phone in the moments leading up to the accident. Yet you have a memory of texting, a very specific memory. Something doesn't add up."

Liam pressed his fingers hard against his temples, as if he could somehow squeeze his thoughts into some semblance of order. "I know. It doesn't make sense, but they must have got it wrong, because I *remember* it. I remember the buzz of the phone on my lap. I remember looking down and seeing it was from Lila. I can still see myself picking up the phone, reading the message, and jabbing back an angry reply." He laughed mirthlessly. "My face was all red and scrunched up while I was texting. I was fucking furious."

"Wait." Allie wrinkled her nose in evident confusion. "That doesn't make sense. What you just said doesn't make sense."

"I know, right?" Liam agreed. "I can't get my head around all this. I feel like I did when I was in the hospital just after the accident. For the first week at least, I don't really remember how long it was, I was in and out of consciousness. I had this morphine drip, and when it squirted into my system it was like I would be dragged down into this sort of whirlpool, a torpor of weird, slow-motion dreams. I feel sort of like that now. Reality is shifting under my feet like the floor in a funhouse. I can't get my balance."

"Oh, my god," Allie said softly. "That's *it*, Liam.

"What's it?"

"It didn't happen. The texting. The argument. None of it actually happened. At least, not in the moments leading up to the accident."

"What?" Liam tilted his head at Allie. "What're you talking about? I remember it. That's what I'm telling you."

Allie shook her head decisively. "You *believe* the whole texting thing took place while you were driving, but that doesn't make it so." When Liam opened his mouth to protest, Allie stopped him with a raised hand, her tone increasingly urgent. "No, please, just hear me out, okay?"

Liam closed his mouth and nodded, mentally reaching for the lifeline Allie was dangling toward him with her words, though he didn't yet understand their meaning.

"It didn't happen, Liam," she repeated. "You must have dreamed it."

"What?"

Allie rushed on. "First off, that bizarre argument with Lila sounds pretty implausible, though admittedly, I don't know the girl. But what you said about *seeing* yourself *is* impossible. It has to be a false memory. A morphine-induced false memory." Her voice rose with excitement. "I've heard of that happening. That has to be it!"

Liam's confusion must have shown on his face, because Allie persisted, "You said, 'My face was all red and scrunched up while I was texting.' You can't *see* your own face, Liam. Except in a dream."

Liam was suddenly lightheaded, as if the coffee he'd been sipping was actually pure grain alcohol.

Allie jumped excitedly from her chair. "Don't you see, Liam? You were in that hospital, half out of your mind from pain and drugs. It was a dream, not a memory at all. It's the only explanation that makes sense."

Liam stared at Allie. It was as if she'd jolted his heart with defibrillator paddles. He understood her words, but couldn't quite grab hold of them. What of the persistent nightmares, so vivid, so insistent, so damning? What of the memory, burned like acid on his synapses, of jerking his head up from the phone screen just in time to see the car speeding toward him like an oncoming bullet? What of the deep, hidden wound of his shame at his part in the accident, which had festered and oozed in his psyche for all those long, lonely months?

"I wonder," Allie said, pulling Liam from his thoughts. "Maybe you did text back and forth with Lila, but from your hospital bed, not the car. I mean—" She paused, hesitation on her face.

"What?" Liam said, aware she was onto something, though he couldn't quite catch hold of it. "Go on. Say it."

"Well," Allie said, "you guys were in the middle of breaking up, right? You were still in the hospital, still probably pretty doped up on pain meds. Maybe your brain has somehow intertwined memories of the accident and the breakup, both really traumatic events."

"With a dash of crazy thrown in," Liam said, barking a laugh. "Lila in chains carrying a flogger down the aisle." He shook his head at the absurd image.

The corner of Allie's mouth quirked. "Yeah, there's that. Blame it on the morphine."

"So what you're saying," Liam said slowly, "is that my brain got things scrambled up. Dreams, reality, timing..." He trailed off as the blurred confusion in his mind finally began to sharpen into something clearer.

Lila had come to the hospital several times during that first week, not trying to hide her horror when she saw him hooked up to all that machinery, his eyes nearly swollen shut, tubes and needles everywhere. He had a vague memory of an actual screaming fight at one point, and then she'd stopped coming, instead resorting to texting to express her fears, her worry and her doubts. Finally, she broke off the engagement, ending the text with a sad face emoticon.

Jesus, she'd broken up with him via text. No wonder he'd been slamming his thumbs against the keys in his hurt and fury. He'd carried that hurt for months, worrying it like an empty tooth socket.

Now the last vestige of regret at losing Lila slipped away as Allie gazed at him with a gentle, encouraging smile. The burden of shame he'd carried so long at helping to orphan that man's children dissolved as he stared into Allie's kind, loving eyes. Hope, bright and hot, rose in his chest like a burst of sunlight.

"Oh, my god," he said, his voice a whispered croak as he finally understood the gift Allie had just handed him. "It didn't happen. It *wasn't* my fault. I didn't kill him." Tears were rolling down his cheeks, but he didn't care.

Allie knelt beside him, reaching up to cradle his face. "No, Liam. It wasn't your fault. The eyewitnesses on the scene said you were driving safely in your own lane. As tragic as it was, that man killed himself." She lifted her shoulders, adding, "Who knows, if you hadn't reacted as quickly as you had, swerving away just in time, he might have killed you, too."

Liam reached for Allie's hands and clasped them in his own. He stood from the table, pulling her upright as he did so. Allie, too, had tears on her cheeks, but her eyes were shining, her lips curved into a broad smile.

Happiness and relief rolled up from Liam's toes, traveling through his body and bursting from his lips as a startled laugh. With a whoop of joy, he grabbed Allie around the waist and lifted her into his arms.

~*~

Allie admired the brocade corset, running her finger over one of the stays. The corset was crimson, black piping on the edges and black laces in the back. Liam and she had selected it together at a BDSM clothing boutique and Allie couldn't wait to show it off at Liam's club that night.

They were to meet Matt and Bonnie for dinner first. Allie, who had already secretly given Bonnie Liam's completed birthday gift so he wouldn't see it in advance, planned to give it to him at the restaurant. Hopefully, it would come in handy at the club.

The change in Liam had been marked since their discovery of his false memory. Though she hadn't known him before the accident, she sensed that he hadn't changed so much as returned to his real self, to the person he had been before the drunk driver had shattered his world. He laughed easily and often, and seemed, in spite of his limp, to walk with a lighter step.

The doorbell rang, pulling Allie from her thoughts.

"Can you get that?" Liam called from the bathroom, where he was dressing after his shower.

Allie, still in her T-shirt and shorts, called back, "Sure. Who is it? Are we expecting someone?"

"Maybe it's one of your jewelry inventory packages. Make sure and look through the peephole before you open the door."

Allie padded on bare feet through the living room to the front door. She didn't recall having ordered anything recently for her jewelry business. She had found a wonderful bead and gem store in downtown Portland where she had begun to buy most of her supplies.

She leaned forward and looked through the peephole. She blinked several times, trying to make sense of what, or rather who, was standing there.

With a laugh, Allie pulled open the front door and demanded, "What the heck are you guys doing here? You're not supposed to be here until next month."

Lauren opened her arms and Allie stepped into them, still laughing as they embraced.

Martin, standing just beside Lauren with suitcases in both hands, said, "Lauren told me all about your romantic arrival on Liam's doorstep. We decided it would be fun to do the same thing."

"Hey, guys, glad to see you made it. I was worried you might not get here before we had to leave for dinner." Allie whipped around to face Liam, who stood grinning at them from the hallway.

"You knew about this? You knew they were coming?" she demanded, though she, too, was smiling.

"He not only knew, it was his idea," Lauren said with a laugh.

Liam shrugged. "What can I say? Turnabout is fair play, right?"

"Touché," Allie said with a laugh.

"Well, don't keep us standing here. We're tired and hungry. Show us to our luxury accommodations," Lauren said.

Allie stepped back, inviting their guests into the house. She turned to Liam. "We'll have to change the reservations from four to six. I'll need to call Bonnie. She made the dinner arrangements."

"Already taken care of," Liam said, his expression smug.

"You mean Bonnie and Matt knew they were coming too?"

"They sure did," Liam replied. "In fact, I bounced the idea off them before I talked to Martin. I know how much you've been missing Lauren, and I thought it would be fun for them to come along to Paradise Found. Portland's not like Boston. We don't have that many BDSM clubs, but what we lack in quantity, I can assure you we definitely make up for in quality."

"We can't wait," Martin said. He held up one of the suitcases. "I packed all my toys. Checked 'em right through."

"I bet that made a few eyes pop if yours was one of the checked bags that got a random inspection," Liam laughed.

They showed Lauren and Martin to the small guest room at the back of the house. As they walked down the hall, Liam put his arm around Allie and whispered into her ear, "I hope the surprise was a good one, sweetheart. I wanted to make you happy."

Allie leaned into Liam. "It was definitely a surprise. And, yes, a good one. I'm really happy they're here. Thank you."

The restaurant was small, the atmosphere romantic, the food excellent. The three couples chatted easily and laughed often. When the dinner plates were cleared, the waiter appeared with an ice bucket containing a bottle of champagne, a second waiter with six champagne flutes, which he placed around the table.

Liam glanced quizzically at Allie. She grinned and shrugged. Liam lifted his eyebrows in Matt's direction, but he only smiled back without saying a word.

The waiter popped the champagne and started to fill the glasses.

"I got it, thanks," Matt said, standing and taking the bottle from the waiter, who bowed and moved away from the table. As Matt filled their glasses, he announced, "This champagne is in celebration of the birthday of my very best friend, Liam Riley Byrne. We are so happy to have you in our lives, Liam."

Liam smiled fondly at his friend, clearly touched. "Thanks, buddy.

I'm pretty happy to be here." As they all laughed, he turned his gaze to Allie, his hand finding her thigh beneath the table. "And I have the best possible birthday gift right here beside me."

"Sweet," Martin and Lauren said in unison. Matt and Bonnie just smiled.

Allie's heart glowed with warmth. Liam's light touch on her leg sent a shiver of desire along her spine. As much to distract herself from the sudden thrum in her sex as anything, Allie turned to Liam and said in a voice everyone at the table could hear, "Since it's a night for surprises, I have one more, this one for you, Sir Liam."

She shot a look at Bonnie, who gave a small nod, and leaned over to pull the hidden gift from beneath her chair. Bonnie handed it across the table to Allie, who in turn presented it to Liam.

"Wow, what the heck is that? It's huge," Liam said as he took the long, narrow box into his hands.

"Open it and see," Allie said, butterflies of nervous excitement fluttering in her belly.

Liam stood and set the gift on its end on his chair. He plucked off the red bow and pulled away the shiny white wrapping paper. Laying the box flat across the chair, he lifted the lid and plucked at the tissue paper.

Allie held her breath, praying he would love it as much as she did. If she said so herself, it was one of the best pieces she'd ever made, and certainly the biggest. She'd shown it to Bonnie and Matt before wrapping it, and they'd assured her it was both spectacular and unique, the perfect gift for Liam.

Liam pulled the specially designed walking stick from the box, his mouth falling open as he turned to regard Allie. "It's beautiful," he said with such evident awe she couldn't doubt his sincerity. "I love it."

~*~

As Liam looked from the walking cane to Allie to his other friends, old and new, he felt as if his heart would burst. He was happier than he had ever been. His path this past year, however tortured, had led him to this wonderful girl, to Allie. He loved her in a way he had never loved anyone before, with not only his heart, but with his soul.

The walking stick he now examined in greater detail truly was beautiful, made of a deep, rich wood, the section just below the handle grip wrapped with silver and gold filigree, ruby-red stones set in a pleasing pattern in its delicate web.

He gripped the handle as he placed the cane's tip on the floor. It fit his hand perfectly, and the rubber tip gripped the floor without sliding.

"It's got your initials. You can see them if you look carefully," Allie said excitedly, pointing to the filigree. Sure enough, as Liam examined the finely wrought precious metal, he was able to discern his initials: LRB. "That way," Allie quipped, "you won't get it confused, if someone else has the same cane on the bus."

As they laughed, Bonnie added, "There's more to it. Show him, Allie," she said, excited impatience in her tone. "Show him the best part."

Liam looked quizzically at Allie, who nodded. "Yeah, this part *no* one else will have, even that guy on the bus. It's what's inside, Liam. Like you, there's more to that walking cane than meets the eye. Just give the handle a twist and you'll see."

Deeply intrigued, Liam did as Allie said, noting now the nearly indiscernible break in the wood. He gently twisted the handgrip until it released. Pulling upward, he saw there was something contained in the hollow of the walking cane. Reaching for the leather loop atop it, he pulled a full-length BDSM rattan cane from inside.

"Holy shit," he exclaimed with a laugh. "You hid a cane in a cane. How cool is that?"

"Wow, that's amazing," Martin exclaimed.

"Allie, that's the best thing you've ever made," Lauren agreed enthusiastically. "I see a whole new line of BDSM gear in your future, girlfriend."

Liam slid the BDSM cane back into its grooved slot and screwed the grip back into place. "When did you make this? I never saw you working on it."

Allie shrugged. "Here and there. When you're busy writing a grant, you get as lost in what you're doing as I do when I'm working on a new jewelry design. It wasn't hard to keep the project hidden."

Liam leaned over and kissed Allie's cheek, resisting the urge to do more, since they were, after all, in a restaurant. "Thank you, baby. I know just what to do with it." He flashed a grin.

"And you get to use it tonight, right?" Lauren said eagerly. "Allie told me you guys have been working with the cane. I want to see for myself."

Liam turned to Lauren, still grinning. "Oh, yeah. You can count on it. In fact," he said, looking slowly from Lauren to Allie to Bonnie in turn, "if I have my way, all three of you will get a taste of this cane tonight, right, guys?"

He looked at Martin and Matt, who said in unison, "Oh, yeah."

CHAPTER 13

As the six of them entered the front door of Paradise Found, Liam experienced a peculiar sense of déjà vu. The place looked at once familiar and different, like an old home he used to live in. In a way it *was* like a home, one, until recently, he thought he'd never return to.

The place smelled the same, a peculiar mix of the sandalwood incense the owners liked to burn, combined with wood smoke, sweat, sex and fine leather. While Liam was excited to be back, he was also a little apprehensive. The membership was small, and there was a good chance he would encounter people he knew, people who hadn't seen him since his leg had been shattered and cobbled back together with metal pins and plates.

As Allie, Martin and Lauren exclaimed over the uniqueness of the place, Liam glanced around. There were only about ten people on the first floor, a few of them already engaged in a scene involving a voluptuous woman bound to a table, two men and another woman standing over her dripping hot wax on her naked body. Another group was chatting quietly, two of them seated on a sofa, two others standing at the large stone fireplace, drinks in their hands. He recognized none of them.

Matt, standing beside Liam, said quietly, "It's great to have you back, buddy. I'm so glad you're here tonight."

Liam, gripping the head of his beautiful new walking cane, turned to smile at his best friend. "Thanks, Matt. Me, too."

"You'd never guess from the exterior this is anything but someone's house. How'd they manage that?" Martin asked.

"It is someone's house," Bonnie replied. "It also happens to be a private BDSM club. Notice, we didn't pay anything at the door, and Matt used his key to enter. Officially, we're all just friends of Paradise Found. It's simpler that way. We pay our annual dues, and we can use the space whenever we want—the first two floors, that is. Robert and Darla live on the top floor."

"Robert and Darla?" Allie queried.

"They're the owners," Bonnie replied. "They must be, what, around seventy, Matt?" She looked toward her husband, who nodded. "They both made a ton of money in Silicon Valley and decided to retire here in Portland. Luckily for us, they bought this old, rundown house, and fixed it up. They put a ton of money into restoring it. The first two floors are the club. They're open to members Wednesday through Sunday, from eight o'clock until the last person is done with their scene."

"Speak of the devil," Matt added, nodding toward the approaching couple. "Here they come."

Darla Hemingway glided toward Liam, her hands outstretched. She was still an attractive woman, her silver-white hair held back from her face by tortoiseshell combs on either side of her head, her eyes a vivid blue. She was dressed in her usual outfit of a formfitting, black, full-length satin gown, a jeweled slave collar around her neck.

"Liam, darling," she said, pulling Liam down for a hug. "Bonnie said you would be here tonight." Letting him go, she surveyed him critically. "You look great. I'm furious that you stayed away for so long, but glad you're back."

Her husband appeared a moment later, a tall, thin man, his shoulders slightly stooped. He hadn't aged as well as his wife, but was still a formidable presence, his dark eyes glowing with dominant confidence. He had always reminded Liam of a praying mantis. Robert shook Liam's hand heartily and then introductions were made all around.

"Bonnie said there would be six of you tonight," Darla said. "So we've reserved the lavender room for you."

"Though, of course"—Robert waved his hand expansively over the main play area—"you're welcome to play down here as well. After all"—he placed his hands on Bonnie's and Lauren's backs—"the night is young, and the subs are beautiful."

"If you're planning to change for the evening's play, you can use the ladies' lounge," Darla said, addressing the girls. "Martin, there's a gentlemen's lounge just over there." She gestured toward the changing rooms.

Martin, Matt and Liam had all worn their black leather pants to dinner, disguising their Dom look somewhat with sports jackets. The three girls, however, had worn sexy, slinky dresses. Corsets and slave collars were a little risqué for the Portland dining scene. Liam couldn't wait to see Allie in her new corset.

The guys handed the girls their BDSM clothing from the gear bags, and the women disappeared into the ladies' lounge. Martin, too, excused himself.

Matt turned to Liam. "I'll go get some bottles of water for afterward. Are you still up for the three-couple scene we talked about with Martin?"

"Sure," Liam said. "I might as well jump in with both feet, right?"

"Okay, great," Matt said. "I'll be back in a flash."

"Hey, Matt Wilson, is that you?" someone called from the kitchen.

"One and the same," Matt replied as he disappeared through the kitchen's swinging doors.

Liam remained alone, content to take in the atmosphere of the place, his mind revisiting scenes he'd shared with Lila in every room of the first and second floor of this old house, though it now seemed like a very long time ago, another life.

As if his memory conjured her from thin air, Liam heard Lila's distinctive, low, throaty voice. "Liam Byrne. Is that really you?"

He turned his head slowly, still not entirely convinced he hadn't imagined her.

But it was Lila, all right, clad in a black leather mini-dress, her large, shapely breasts spilling over the top, her smoky blue eyes sultry with promise. Her red hair was piled in a coil on the top of her head, and long earrings shaped like tiny handcuffs dangled from her ears. Though she was every bit as beautiful as he'd remembered, the catch in his throat the sight of her had once engendered was absent.

As he took her in, Liam waited for the punch to his gut, for the pain of the loss he had carried like a knife in his heart for so long to twist. There was no pain, however, not even a whisper. He felt nothing. Nothing, save for mild surprise at seeing her.

"Lila. Hello."

She looked him up and down and smiled that slow, sexy smile he remembered well. "I thought you were in a wheelchair," she said with a lift of perfectly sculpted brows. "But you looked quite intact to my eye. In fact, you look fucking fantastic."

Moving closer, she brushed his arm with her breast, the movement apparently casual, though he was certain it was deliberate. He could smell her perfume, something strong and cloying. He took a step back.

"I'm doing okay," he replied noncommittally. He glanced down at his leg, gripping the beautiful cane Allie had given him a little tighter. "Not quite intact, but doing just fine. How are you?"

"I've missed you," Lila said in a little girl's voice. "After our fight that day at the hospital"—she shrugged, a sad, remorseful look passing over her pretty face—"I was afraid to come back. We"—she swallowed, correcting herself—"*I* said some pretty horrible things. I was ashamed of myself. But I never stopped missing you."

Liam said nothing to this, thinking only that action, or the lack of it, spoke far louder than words.

Lila rubbed her breast on his arm again, and once more Liam stepped away. "It's really fabulous to see you again," she persisted. "Maybe we could get toget—"

"What do you think, Master Liam?" Lauren said, her loud voice causing both Lila and Liam to jump. He turned to look in the direction of the sound, relieved that he wouldn't have to rebuff Lila, who had always enjoyed a scene, not necessarily the good kind.

Lauren pointed to Allie, who stood beside her, breathtakingly stunning in her crimson corset, her long, lovely legs clad in sheer black stockings, matching red heels on her feet. "She cleans up nice, huh?" Lauren said.

"She does indeed. You look pretty good, too," Liam said chivalrously. In fact, all three women were stunning. Lauren, her long blond hair flowing, was clad in a skimpy black leather bustier with zippers on either side, black stockings held up by garters, her feet in stiletto heels. Bonnie with her short, dark hair and large dark eyes, had painted her lips a shiny cherry red. She had changed into a see-through, pale gold satin gown, her nipples visible beneath the sheer fabric. Her outfit contrasted nicely with the simple but elegant black leather collar that dipped in a V toward her breasts.

Bonnie, clearly recognizing Lila, flashed a worried glance in Liam's direction, but Liam just smiled, sending her a telepathic message not to worry.

He turned his gaze to Allie, who glanced from Lila to him and smiled tentatively, a question in her eyes, though she said nothing.

Drawn as if she were a magnet and he made of metal, Liam moved toward her and put his arm around her shoulders, pulling her close. "You look beautiful," he murmured into her ear.

"Who's this?" Lila said, her usually throaty voice suddenly shrill. Liam jerked his head in her direction, startled to realize he'd forgotten all about her.

"I'm sorry," he said, dropping his arm from Allie's shoulders to her waist. "Allie," he said, "this is Lila, an old friend of mine."

Allie's eyes widened in obvious surprise, and then a hint of a smile moved over her lips. "Nice to meet you, Lila," she said demurely, as if she had no idea who Lila was, or rather had once been, in Liam's life.

Liam glanced back at the woman who had smashed his heart into pieces, abandoning him when he had needed her most. For a second, he considered introducing Allie as the love of his life, as the woman he was going to marry. But he pushed the uncharitable thought away, aware it was petty and unkind. All the anger, all the sorrow and the hurt, while he hadn't forgotten it, no longer had a place in his life. It no longer served him. Indeed, it never had.

Now that he had had the time and the perspective to work through what had happened between them, he was grateful for Lila's defection. She had saved them both from a relationship that would probably have ended in misery and divorce. Theirs had been a tempestuous, difficult relationship, one that seemed to thrive on discord and then intense, passionate makeup sex. It was, he thought now, a teenagers' affair, not a connection between loving, caring adults.

These thoughts passed through his mind in only a few seconds. But it was long enough for him to hold his tongue and instead say simply, "Lila, this is Allie. Allie Swift."

Matt and Martin appeared a moment later, and if Matt was surprised to see Lila, he didn't show it. She drifted away shortly thereafter, announcing she had a scene scheduled with a famous Australian whip maker, which, Liam had no doubt, was true.

The six of them went upstairs, the men carrying the gear bags over their shoulders. They entered what had once been the master bedroom of the old house. The lavender room was aptly named, the walls painted that color, the recovery sofa and matching wingback chairs in the corner upholstered in a darker purple.

The room contained a St. Andrew's cross, a bondage table, a set of stocks and a portable wooden suspension rack, courtesy of Robert's considerable handyman skills. A full-size bed had been placed parallel to the wall, covered only with a fitted sheet.

Matt put the bottled water in the mini refrigerator in the corner of the room while the rest of them took in the space. "This is amazing," Martin said, turning in a slow circle.

"This whole club is amazing," Allie agreed, the admiration clear in her tone. "This is way better than anything I've ever been to in Boston, right, Lauren?" she said, turning to her friend.

"Uh, yeah," Lauren agreed. "Way, way better. There are no weird, lost-looking loser guys with a latex fetish, trolling for subs, without the least clue what they would do with one if they got her."

"But we know what to do, don't we, guys?" Martin said with a laugh.

"I hope it involves that cool suspension rack," Lauren replied without missing a beat.

"Not tonight," Matt interjected. "Tonight we have something special planned for you three lovelies."

"That's right," Liam said, excited at the prospect. "We won't use rope or chain to tie you down. Instead, you'll hold yourselves still and in position, offering your bodies for our pleasure and your erotic pain."

"Ooh," Allie said softly. Just the sound of her voice was enough to send a jolt of electricity directly to Liam's cock.

Martin closed the door of the room and glanced to Matt, who turned to the three women. They stood clustered together, their lovely faces a study in excitement and nervous anticipation. "Tonight," Matt said, taking up the thread, "we are going to test the limits of your submissive obedience. As Liam said, you won't be bound. You'll maintain your position purely by force of will."

"That's right," Martin added. "We each decided on a favorite toy tonight. I'm going to employ my trusty single tail"—Lauren executed a little happy dance—"Matt will use his paddle—"

"Bonnie's paddle," Matt interjected with an evil grin.

"Bonnie's paddle," Martin amended. "And Liam, naturally, will bring into play the new cane his sub girl presented to him this evening."

"We don't want you to mess up those beautiful outfits," Liam added, his cock throbbing in anticipation. "While you girls strip, we'll set out the toys."

"Shoes, too," Matt added. "You'll need your balance for this scene."

All three of the guys stole glances at their women as they undressed. At the same time, they unzipped their gear bags and removed their chosen toys, along with the sleep mask blindfolds Matt had brought along, placing them on the counter provided for the purpose.

"For this session," Matt said, standing in front of the naked women like a drill sergeant overseeing his soldiers, "the three of you will stand in a circle facing each other. You will lift your arms over your heads and hold hands during the entire session. You will plant your feet in an at-ease position, asses thrust out. To help you focus and stop you from anticipating, you will be blindfolded. The three of us will move from girl to girl behind you. You'll be paddled, whipped and caned as it pleases us."

"Before we begin," Liam added, "you will each remind us of your safeword." He turned first to Matt's sub. "Bonnie?"

"Apple, Sir," Bonnie replied calmly.

"Lauren?"

"Rosebud, Sir," Lauren squeaked, and then giggled.

"Allie?"

"Diamond, Sir."

"Good," Liam said. "Do you have any questions before we begin?"

"No, Sir," all three girls replied at once, causing everyone in the room to laugh.

Liam was happy. It was wonderful to be with friends, good friends whom he trusted and admired. While there was levity, all six of them were serious players in the scene, and he was excited for this opportunity. He was returning to a life he had, until recently, thought was behind him. It felt good to be back.

Bonnie, Allie and Lauren stood in a circle as directed, reaching up to clasp hands. The men moved behind them, adjusting a leg here and a bottom there, until all three women stood properly, feet apart, asses out.

Finally, they slipped the black satin sleep masks over the subs' eyes. The three men moved behind the girls, stopping to cup their breasts or slip their hands between their legs. The subs remained still and silent as the men touched them, though their erect nipples and moist pussies gave them away.

Both Matt and Martin, Liam couldn't help but observe, sported raging erections just as he did. But they all knew good things came to those who waited.

At a nod from Matt, they picked up their chosen implements from the counter, each assuming a position behind his partner. Allie gasped at the first stroke of Liam's cane, but then settled down.

He tapped lightly, warming her skin gradually, his focus entirely on her. The room was silent, save for leather and wood striking flesh, and the women's increasingly rapid breathing. At another nod from Matt, the three men shifted their positions, Liam now behind Bonnie, Martin behind Allie.

The women began to cry out in turn, yelps and gasps as the paddle hit especially hard, or the whip caught one of them just so, or the cane marked their flesh with a beautiful welt. Slowly, the guys moved around the circle of subs, each man focused on his task. Soon all three bare asses were marked, welts from the cane and small angry dashes from the whip appearing on flesh reddened by the hard wooden paddle.

Liam's cock throbbed, his balls aching, his heart pulsing in time to the syncopated pants and cries of the subs as the Doms intensified their erotic beatings. Though he tried to focus on all three women equally, Liam's attention was drawn continually to his girl. Her face was flushed, her lips parted, her hair wild as she tossed her head and gasped at each new stroke of the cane, kiss of the whip and smack of the paddle.

The other two subs, he managed to observe, were equally affected, their chests heaving, their breathing ragged. Somehow, through it all, the girls kept their fingers entwined, their heads bowed toward each other as if in prayer.

Matt was now behind Bonnie, Martin behind Lauren, Liam behind Allie. By some silent accord, they no longer rotated. Liam placed his hand on the back of Allie's neck and gave it a reassuring squeeze. Leaning close, he said softly, "You're doing beautifully, sub Allie. I want to take you even further than we went the last time. Does that suit you, sub girl?"

"Yes, Sir," Allie breathed without even a moment's hesitation. "Yes, please, Sir."

Liam stepped back and flicked the cane several times against Allie's already tortured flesh. Long lines of white appeared against the reddened skin, rapidly darkening as the blood rushed to their aid. He struck the tender flesh where her ass met her thigh, drawing a low, feral moan from her lips.

Moving slightly to the side, he angled his wrist and let the cane fly through the air, connecting with the fleshy center of both cheeks.

He forgot where he was, or who was watching, his focus now entirely on Allie. He painted welts in parallel lines and crisscross patterns over every inch of those perfect globes, the cane beating in time to Allie's breathless, tortured cries.

Then it began to happen: Allie's cries quieted and then ceased, her head falling slowly back as her breathing deepened and slowed. She pulled her hands from the other two, and Bonnie and Lauren let her go.

As if on cue, from behind, Martin drew Lauren against him, while Matt held Bonnie in his arms. The guys removed their subs' blindfolds. The four of them were now watching Liam and Allie, waiting for them to continue.

Returning his attention fully to his sub girl, Liam resumed the caning, delivering a strong, searing stroke that left tiny droplets of blood in its wake.

Allie didn't cry out. She didn't even moan. She stood as still and graceful as a statue, the very essence of submissive grace. Awestruck, Liam aimed the cane once more. This welt, too, beaded with blood, shiny red against the darker mottled red of her well-beaten ass.

While a part of Liam, the primal, dominant beast in him, ached to continue, he knew it was time to stop. Allie was no longer in a position to use her safeword. Her spirit was soaring somewhere he could only follow from a distance, as if she were a kite wheeling wildly overhead, tethered to the earth solely by the strings of his responsibility to keep her safe.

He set down the cane and moved to stand in front of his flying sub girl. Reaching around her head, he gently removed the blindfold. Her eyes remained closed, her breathing still deep and even, as if she were asleep while standing up.

He placed his hands on her shoulders. "Allie," he said softly, "I'm here with you. Take as long as you need." He kissed her lightly on the lips. Then he waited, his hands still on her shoulders, as if anchoring her in place while she soared.

After another minute or so, during which everyone in the room remained completely silent, Allie opened her eyes and blinked several times.

Then she smiled, the radiance of her smile reaching her eyes, which danced and sparkled as they regained their focus. "That," she said emphatically as Liam stepped away to let the others see she had returned to the land of the living, "Was. Totally. Fucking. Awesome."

"Girlfriend," Lauren said from within Martin's embrace from behind her, "I never thought I'd see the day when you would not only submit to a cane, but fly from the experience. I agree with your assessment. Totally. Fucking. Awesome."

"You should see *your* butt, babe," Martin said to Lauren. "Definitely worth a Facebook status update."

Matt whispered something in his wife's ear and she rewarded him with a beatific smile.

Allie reached back to touch her bottom, wincing as she lightly traced her welts. With a startled cry, she brought her hand to her face and stared down at her fingers. "I'm bleeding!"

"You are," Liam agreed calmly. "You took quite a caning, Allie, not to mention a whipping and a paddling. Your marks are beautiful."

"Hey, Liam," Matt called from where he stood with Bonnie. "Did you bring that miracle ointment with you? These girls are in need of some aftercare."

"I never leave home without it," Liam quipped. He moved toward the counter, barely noticing his limp as he walked without the use of his cane. Since the stunning realization that he'd had zero responsibility for that man's death, the pain in his leg had somehow diminished. He hadn't needed to use the pills even once since the amazing revelation.

They had the women lie side-by-side on their stomachs across the bed, each Dom ministering to his sub. When they were properly tended to, the women rose from the bed, each accepting a bottle of water.

While they drank, Martin observed, "I don't know about you guys, but whipping these three gorgeous babes has given me a serious case of blue balls. We've got this private room here. I think our subbies should thank their Masters properly with a little cock worship. You guys down with that?"

"Shit, yeah," Matt rejoined enthusiastically.

Liam met Allie's eye. She gave a small nod of approval, a devilish smile curving her lips.

"Count me in," Liam said with a broad grin.

Still naked, the women knelt prettily in front of their men. All three eagerly opened their flies and pulled out their cocks. Liam didn't try to stifle his moan of pure pleasure as Allie's hot mouth closed over his shaft, her cool fingers cradling his balls.

There was too much pent-up lust for any of them to last long, and it was over way too quickly. Their task easily accomplished, the girls sat back on their heels, each with a satisfied look on her face.

As the guys tucked themselves back into place, Lauren piped up, "What about us? I like a little pleasure with my pain, hmmm?" She cupped her full breasts suggestively, her tongue moving seductively over her lower lip.

Martin grinned. "You little slut. You had your beating; now you want to come too?"

Lauren stuck out her tongue at her boyfriend.

"I have an idea," Matt said. "Let's have them masturbate. All three of them at once while we watch."

"That might result in another round of cock sucking," Bonnie said with a laugh.

"And you have a problem with that?" Matt said to his wife with a lift of his eyebrows.

"Absolutely not, Sir," Bonnie said emphatically, still smiling.

"Let's not bother with permission, right, guys?" Matt suggested. "It'll get too confusing."

"Agreed," Liam said, and Martin, too, nodded his consent.

The three women lay down carefully on their backs on the bed, their heads toward the wall, their beautiful, bare pussies on full display.

Allie was sandwiched between the other two. They all shifted and winced a little as their tortured bottoms made contact with the mattress. Once settled, legs bent, knees spread, they exchanged glances with each other, sharing secret, telepathic communications with their eyes.

Liam watched, entranced with their beauty and fascinated at the differences in style as each girl rubbed and stroked herself. Lauren was the first to come in a series of low, animal grunts, her face twisted in a sexual grimace, her eyes squeezed tight. Bonnie was next, her dark eyes fixed on Matt's as she took herself to completion with a long, trembling sigh.

Allie was left, still stroking and rubbing, her face a mask of concentration. Liam experienced a sudden qualm, recalling her past history and her difficulty in orgasming on command, especially with others watching.

At a gesture from Liam, the other two girls pulled themselves to a sitting position. He lifted his chin toward the guys, who also correctly interpreted his silent communication. They stepped forward and extended their hands to their girls, who allowed themselves to be pulled upright, leaving Allie alone on the mattress.

Liam sat on the mattress beside her. He placed his hand on her throat, sliding his thumb and forefinger in place just below her jaw. "Come for me, sub Allie," he murmured with soft but quiet insistence. He tightened his grip around her throat, his fingers sending a primal message of dominance that made her gasp, her eyes flying open, the pupils dilating as she stared at him.

Almost at once, she began to tremble, her eyes locked on his, her breath now a pant, her fingers flying. With a cry, she bucked, her hips lifting from the bed, her hand moving furiously between her legs. Then she collapsed back against the mattress, her hand still buried between her slender thighs.

There was a hush for a moment, and then everyone began to clap and laugh. Allie's eyes flew open once more, splashes of red moving over cheeks already flushed from orgasm. She met Liam's eye, and he smiled widely at her, lifting his thumb in approval. She sat up and tossed back her hair, her natural sass returning. "What? You've never seen a girl come before?"

~*~

The six of them sat at a table in the club's kitchen, drinking orange juice over crushed ice as they talked over the incredible scene. All agreed it had been a phenomenal success, with Allie its star performer. Though she was embarrassed to be the focus of so much attention, Allie couldn't deny she was also pleased, and more than a little thrilled to have been a part of it all.

She couldn't remember ever being happier in her life. Liam sat beside her, his hand light on her thigh, his eyes warm with love each time their gazes met.

There was a natural lull in the conversation, and then Liam tapped lightly against his glass with his fingernail. "Ladies and gentlemen," he said with a grin, "if I may have your attention please."

They all regarded him expectantly, Allie included.

"Allie isn't the only one with a surprise gift tonight. I have one of my own." Liam reached into the duffel under his chair and brought out a small oblong box wrapped in thick blue paper, a white bow affixed at its center. He handed the box to Allie.

Excited and intrigued, Allie pulled at the paper, tearing it away. She opened the lid, expecting a necklace. But when she lifted the tissue paper, she saw, not a necklace, but a beautiful leather collar, dyed a rich burgundy red. There was a delicate padlock at its center made of high-quality rose gold, fashioned in the shape of a heart. The tiny key was still in its lock.

She lifted the collar from the box and held it up for the others to see. As they all voiced their admiration and approval, Allie turned to her Dom. "Oh, Liam," she exclaimed. "It's beautiful. I've never seen anything so lovely." She stroked the impossibly soft leather, her neck actually tingling with the need to feel it against her skin.

"I had it made by the leather master who did Bonnie's collar," Liam said, beaming happily. "It came out great, right?"

"Master Taggart surpassed himself with that one," agreed Matt. "Bonnie, I'm going to have to get you a new collar. That thing is gorgeous."

"I like this one just fine," Bonnie said, fingering her collar. "But I'd be happy to have a second one," she added with a laugh.

"I want one," Lauren said with a mock pout. She turned to Martin. "Get me one of those, darling."

"Yes, ma'am," Martin replied with a laugh. "Though that's *Sir* darling to you." He turned to the others with a sardonic shrug. "Let 'em come, and it's all over."

Ignoring the banter, Allie handed her beautiful collar to Liam. She leaned her head toward him and lifted her hair. Liam placed the soft leather collar around her neck, buckling it into place behind her head.

Allie sat back, deeply content. She stroked the soft leather and touched the delicate, heart shaped padlock.

Liam reached toward her and plucked the small key from its lock. "I'll hold onto this for safekeeping," he said. His eyes softening, he reached for her face and stroked her cheek with two fingers. "You already have the key to my heart."

Available at Romance Unbound Publishing

(http://romanceunbound.com)

A Lover's Call
A Princely Gift
A Test of Love
Accidental Slave
Alternative Treatment
Beyond the Compound
Binding Discoveries
Blind Faith
Brokered Submission
Cast a Lover's Spell
Caught: Punished by Her Boss
Claiming Kelsey
Closely Held Secrets
Club de Sade
Confessions of a Submissive
Dare to Dominate
Dream Master
Enslaved
Face of Submission
Finding Chandler
Forced Submission
Frog
Golden Angel
Golden Boy
Golden Man
Handyman
Heart of Submission
Heart Thief
Hunted
Island of Temptation
Jewel Thief
Julie's Submission
Lara's Submission
Masked Submission

No Safeword
Obsession: Girl Abducted
Odd Man Out
Our Man Friday
Pleasure Planet
Polar Reaction
Princess
Safe in His Arms
Sarah's Awakening
Secrets
Seduction of Colette
Slave Academy
Slave Castle
Slave Gamble
Slave Girl
Slave Island
Slave Jade
Sold into Slavery
Stardust
Sub for Hire
Submission in Paradise
Submission Times Two
Switch
Switching Gears
Texas Surrender
The Auction
The Compound
The Contract
The Cowboy Poet
The Inner Room
The Keyholder
The Master
The Solitary Knights of Pelham Bay
The Story of Owen
The Toy
Tough Boy
Tracy in Chains
True Kin Vampire Tales:
Sacred Circle
Outcast

CONNECT WITH CLAIRE

Newsletter: http://tinyurl.com/o6tu4eu

Website: http://clairethompson.net

Romance Unbound Publishing: http://romanceunbound.com

Twitter: http://twitter.com/CThompsonAuthor

Facebook: http://www.facebook.com/ClaireThompsonauthor

Manufactured by Amazon.ca
Bolton, ON